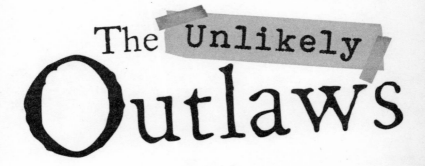

The Unlikely Outlaws

The Unlikely Outlaws

(Sir) PHILIP ARDAGH

Conkers

First published in 2015 in Great Britain by
Barrington Stoke Ltd
18 Walker Street, Edinburgh, EH3 7LP

www.barringtonstoke.co.uk

The Green Men of Gressingham text © 2002 Philip Ardagh
The Red Dragons of Gressingham text © 2008 Philip Ardagh
The Black Knight of Gressingham text © 2015 Philip Ardagh
All other text © 2015 Philip Ardagh
Illustrations © 2015 Tom Morgan-Jones

A CIP catalogue record for this book is available
from the British Library upon request

ISBN: 978-1-78112-371-3

Printed in Great Britain by Clays Ltd, St Ives plc

To

The powerful who help the powerless,

the strong who help the weak,

the rich who help the poor,

and all those who stand up for justice.

ADRIAN DONGLE

Dear Mrs Hendrix

My name is Adrian Dongle and I publish children's books. I am a big fan of Philip Ardagh's stories.

A few weeks ago, I met Sir Philip at a cake-eating competition and asked him if he'd be interested in writing a book for me.

He had his hands (and mouth) full at the time and said that I should get in touch with him through you. He mentioned something about really wanting to write a book about some little green men. (At least, I think that's what he said. There was lots of chewing and crumbs.)

Would it be possible to arrange a meeting?

Very best wishes

Adrian Dongle

Adrian Dongle
Publisher

Sir Philip

What do you want to do about this?

Do you really want to write a book about little green men?

Do you want a meeting?

Dotty

Dotty,

I don't remember Dongle but I do remember the cakes.

I have no idea WHAT he's talking about.

Little green men? I have NO interest in writing about little green ones, big purple ones OR medium-sized ones with yellow spots.

IS HE MAD?

P.A.

GLE

Dotty,

I don't re
rememb

I have
about

Lit
in

P

oks. I

ng a

at I

e
re

ig

Mr Adrian Dongle
Dongle & Dongle Publishers Ltd
Dongle House
The High Street
Little Biglington

A
Pu

AH

~ ARDAGH HOUSE ~

Dear Mr Dongle

Thank you for your recent letter. Sir Philip remembers your meeting at the cake-eating competition with great fondness. (He has some of the cake wrappers stuck in a special scrapbook.)

Unfortunately, he has no memory of saying that he wanted to write about aliens, little green ones or otherwise.

Would you be interested in meeting him to discuss other book ideas?

Yours sincerely

Dotty Hendrix

Dotty Hendrix (Mrs)

FROM THE DESK OF
ADRIAN DONGLE

Dear Mrs Hendrix

I'm delighted that Sir Philip recalls our meeting.

I'm sorry that I misunderstood what he said between huge bites of cake.

I would very much like to meet up with Sir Philip to talk about any ideas he might have. Could we do this sooner rather than later because I have to fly to America next month?

Thank you.

Fingers crossed!

Very best wishes

Adrian Dongl

Adrian Dongle
Publisher

Sir Philip,

As you can see from his letter, Mr Dongle wants:

1. to hear your ideas
2. to meet up soon

Interested?

Dotty

Dotty,

Not fair. How come HE gets to go to America? I haven't been to America for ages. And we're out of bananas. I had the last one when I was watching that Australian antiques cookery programme during my lunch-break. Please buy a big bunch on the way back from collecting my dry-cleaning.

Thank you.

P.A.

P - You still haven't answered my question. D

Do you know what? Something I've been wanting to write about for AGES is a band of Robin-Hood-and-His-Merry-Men-type outlaws. Maybe I could suggest that? It would be FUN.

What I can't decide is whether they should be GOOD outlaws or BAD ones.

Yes, please arrange a meeting with Adam. And make sure he takes me to lunch. I like lunch.

P.A.

His name is ADRIAN not ADAM

Will do. Dotty

Dear Mr Dongle

I'm pleased to say that Sir Philip is very excited by the idea of writing a Robin-Hood-type tale. He said that it would be fun, and he even wrote the word 'FUN' in capital letters. (He usually only uses capital letters if he's written me a note when he's annoyed, such as when I forget to buy more bananas on the way back from collecting his dry-cleaning.) Would you be interested?

He is eager to meet as soon as possible to discuss the idea. Would next Wednesday be possible? He could meet you at lunchtime.

Yours sincerely

Dotty Hendrix

Dotty Hendrix (Mrs)

FROM THE DESK OF
ADRIAN DONGLE

Dear Mrs Hendrix

Wednesday would be perfect.

I've booked a table at The Fat Chef for one o'clock. I look forward to seeing Sir Philip then.

Very best wishes

Adrian Dongle

Adrian Dongle
Publisher

Dotty, Had a jolly good six-course lunch and took plenty of after-dinner mints to eat on the train ride home.

When I told Alan the name I'd come up with for the band of merry men was THE GREEN MEN OF GRESSINGHAM, he got even more excited.

He said they must have been the green men I was talking about at the cake-eating contest. Not LITTLE ones!

I'll start writing it tomorrow. Please get me a fresh supply of paper and pencils and some more bananas.

Thank you, P.A.

His name is
ADRIAN
not ALAN

Will do. Dotty

AH
ARDAGH HOUSE

Dear ~~Alex~~ Adrian,

Here it is: THE GREEN MEN OF GRESSINGHAM.

I had such fun writing this I even gave up watching my favourite Australian antiques cookery programme so I could work through my lunch-breaks every day.

Hope you like it too.

Happy reading.

Philip

The Green Men of
GRESSINGHAM

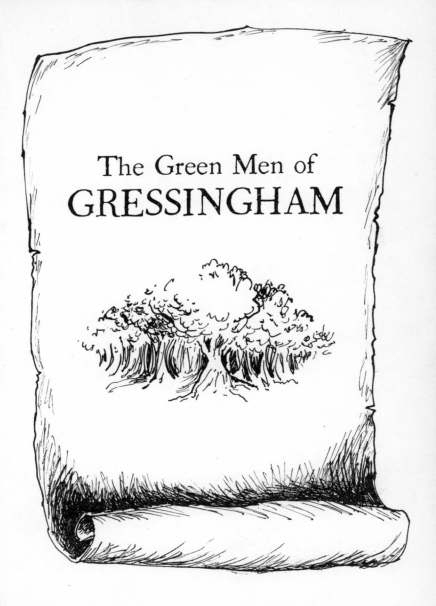

Meet the Green Men of Gressingham, a medieval band of outlaws dressed in brown. Brown? Well, yes. It's cheaper than green and hides the dirt better. There's Big Jim, Friendly, Fidget and many more ... all led by their mysterious masked mistress, Robyn-in-the-Hat.

Chapter 1

INTO THE UNKNOWN

Tom Dashwood was up before the cock crowed, which wasn't as early as you might imagine because it was a Friday. The cock always had a lie-in on Fridays. It was still pretty early, though, and the servants had only been up five hours when Tom appeared in the great hall. The straw the servants used for their bedding had long since been cleared away, and Cook had laid some breakfast on the long table.

Tom and his family didn't usually have breakfast together, but this was no ordinary morning. This was because a big man with a rather squishy hat had arrived at their manor house the day before. His name was Able Morris and he'd been sent by Tom's uncle, Lord Dashwood, to bring Tom back to Dashwood Castle. There the boy could train to be a page.

Training to be a page was the first step towards becoming a real, live knight. No wonder Tom had been so excited that he'd hardly slept. Ever since he could remember, he'd been looking forward to going to Dashwood Castle to train to be one of his uncle's knights. And now, at long last, that day had come. He'd spent much of the night imagining himself in sword fights or jousts with the sound of horses' hooves and cheering crowds thundering in his ears.

It was Tom's mother, Lady Dashwood, who thought that a farewell breakfast would be a nice idea. It was one last chance to spend a little time with her son before he left. She was very pleased for him but, at the same time, she was sad to see him go. Most mums are like that.

Because it was so early they all drank small beer instead of the strong stuff. (They never drank water  from their well because it was usually a horrible brown colour and tasted like mud. They always drank beer instead, and 'small beer' was the weakest.) Tom ate thick slices of bread full of seeds and had an apple too.

Now it came to it, his mother wasn't

hungry so she chewed her hanky instead. She had big bags under her eyes and looked as though she'd also been awake all night. That was because she *had* been awake all night. She'd been thinking of her little boy leaving home.

"I propose a toast," said Tom's father, Sir Simon Dashwood, rising to his feet. "To my son, Thomas, on his first step on the road to chivalry and honour!"

"Chivalry and honour," agreed Able Morris, and everyone raised their goblets or tankards to their lips. Tom felt so proud that his face glowed a very nice shade of red.

"We must take our leave of you now, Sir Simon," said Able Morris. "Your son and I have a long journey and a dusty road ahead of us."

Everyone, including the servants, went to the front of the manor house to see Tom on his way. Lady Dashwood's hanky wasn't only wet from the chewing now, but also from her tears.

"Be brave and true, Tom," she said, because that's the sort of thing mothers said to sons going off to become pages.

Tom's father gave him a hug, then Able Morris leaned forward on his huge horse, grabbed him by the hand and yanked him up onto the back of the beast. Tom now sat behind him. Tom secretly hoped that Able Morris didn't ride too fast because there was no way that he could put his arms around the man's waist to hold on. It was far too wide!

Able Morris turned his head (squishy hat and all) to look at Tom. "It is time to leave,

Master Thomas!" With the words 'goodbye'
and 'good luck' ringing in their ears, Tom, Able
and Able's horse Ferdy began the journey to
Dashwood Castle.

*

To begin with, they passed through places
familiar to Tom. These were places he'd been
to with his father: the village with its noise and
smells, the monastery with the silent monks and
their scratchy pens, the field where the carnival
came each year.

Soon they were travelling through
countryside Tom had only ever seen in the
distance. He turned in the saddle and could no
longer see his home, though he could still make

out the very top of the local church tower, poking above the trees.

"We'll be coming to Gressingham Forest soon, Master Thomas," said Able. "There be outlaws in that place, so don't say a word and hold on tight, for a quick escape may be the order of the day."

Tom felt a mixture of fear and excitement. They'd only been gone less than a day and already he was in the middle of an adventure! Up ahead, the track disappeared into the forest, thick with trees. Tom's mouth went dry as Able flicked the reins and Ferdy trotted into the forest. On they went, and on, then further still.

Tom kept looking from left to right, peering into the darkness of the thick undergrowth. *Outlaws won't be interested in the likes of us*, he thought. *They'll only be interested in rich people wearing expensive jewellery or merchants with bags of gold coins* ... Wrong!

There was a noise up ahead. It sounded like the hoot of an owl, but Tom knew enough to know that owls didn't hoot in the daytime. It must be a signal!

It was.

Moments later, Tom and Able were surrounded by a gang of men dressed in brown. The tallest man Tom had ever seen in his life strode towards them. He was so tall that his head

was higher off the ground than Able's, and Able was sitting on a horse!

"We have visitors!" laughed the man, his voice deep and booming. "Let's make them welcome, men."

Next to him stood one of the smallest men Tom had ever seen, which made the tall man seem even taller still. Before Tom quite knew what was happening – let alone had a chance to respond – he found himself being dragged off the horse and stuffed into a sack.

*

The outlaws must have had a selection of sacks in all shapes and sizes, because they found one big enough for Able Morris too. He was a lot heavier and struggled a lot more than Tom, so it took six outlaws to get him in his sack – and not before they had to stuff his squishy hat in his mouth to stop him shouting "Thieves!" and "Murderers!" and a few other things far too rude for me to write down here.

Tom could hear all this going on, but couldn't see it because he was already in his own (smaller) sack, which had been tied shut at the top with rope. It was quite comfortable as outlaws' sacks went. The material wasn't too thick, so the evening light could still filter through it. It wasn't made of that itchy material which makes you want to scratch half the time, either.

Tom could have done with a cushion in there and a window would have been nice, but

Tom didn't have too much to complain about except, of course, for the fact that he'd been kidnapped by outlaws and put in a sack in the first place. If he didn't manage to come up with an escape plan, he might never get to be a knight after all.

After Tom had grown tired of shouting "Let me out!" and was actually beginning to think that a short snooze might not be a bad idea, he felt the sack being lifted. The next moment, he found the end being untied and he was tipped out onto the mossy ground.

Tom took in his surroundings, blinking in the light. He was somewhere deep in the forest, sitting in the middle of a circle of outlaws, armed with staffs, bows and arrows.

"Who are you?" he demanded. "And what

have you done with Able Morris?"

The very tall man laughed. "We're the
outlaws and you're the prisoner, so we get to ask
the questions," he bellowed. This made the other
men (for they were all men) burst out laughing
too. The smallest of them tripped over a tree
root.

"My name is Tom Dashwood," said
Tom, pulling himself up to his full
height and dusting himself down.
"My parents are Sir Simon and
Lady Dashwood ..."

"Which means that Lord
Dashwood of Dashwood Castle be
your uncle!" said a rather jolly-
looking outlaw, dressed like the
others all in brown.

"Yes he be ... Yes he is," said Tom proudly. "Now, I think you'd better let me and Able Morris go before Uncle Alf sends an army of knights out to look for me ..."

"Oooh! I'm quaking in my brown boots," said the tall man, rudely.

"Quake all you like but you're certainly too cowardly to tell me your own names!" snapped Tom.

That wiped the smile off the tall man's face. "No one calls Big Jim a coward," he said. "That's my name, Big Jim."

"I'm Squat," said the smallest man, pulling himself up to his fullest height (which wasn't much), "and we are the Green Men of Gressingham."

Tom looked at the men who surrounded him. Although they came in all different shapes and sizes, they all wore similar clothes.

"The Green Men of Gressingham?" asked Tom. There were nods and murmurs of "yes". "Then why are you all dressed in brown?"

"Brown material is cheaper than green and hides the dirt better," said the jolly one. "We don't get much time to wash our clothes, being dastardly outlaws. My name is Friendly."

He held out his hand for Tom to shake.

Shaking hands was a way for one person to show another he had no weapons hidden in his palm – and the actual shaking would make any hidden daggers fall out of their sleeves.

Despite the rather unfortunate circumstances, Tom couldn't help liking Friendly. He even looked friendly. Tom shook his hand. "I do think it would be better for all of us if you let me and Able Morris go," he said.

"You're a stubborn one, aren't you?" said Big Jim. "What is your business in Gressingham Forest, Thomas Dashwood?"

"I'm on my way to the castle," said Tom. He saw no point in hiding the truth. "I'm going to learn to be a knight."

"The castle be a bad place," said Friendly. He looked sad at the thought of it.

"For robbers and outlaws, perhaps," said Tom, "but not for honest people."

"And when were you last at the castle?" demanded another of the Green Men of Gressingham. This one was called Fidget.

"I've never been," Tom confessed.

"Then how do you know what goes on

there?" demanded Fidget. "I'm telling you, boy, terrible things happen there. Terrible!"

"We can't blame the boy for his uncle's crimes," said Friendly, walking around Tom in a circle. "If he's never even been to the castle, I say we let him go!" Now Tom really liked him. (I can't think why.)

Hooray! thought Tom.

"And I say we hold him to ransom," said Big Jim. "His lordship's nephew might fetch a pretty penny."

Boo! Hiss! thought Tom.

"It's not pennies we're after but bags of gold!" cried another. (This was Lanky who was almost as tall as Big Jim but very thin, like a runner bean.)

"It's decided then," said Big Jim. "We keep

the boy and set the fat man free. He can take a message to Lord Dashwood that we are holding his nephew a prisoner."

"That's up to the boss, not us," said Friendly. The others fell silent.

All Tom could hear was Able Morris struggling in his sack, under a far-off tree. "I thought you *were* the boss," said Tom, facing the enormous Big Jim.

"Er, no," said Big Jim. "I'm only in charge until Robyn-in-the-Hat returns."

"And Robyn is your leader?"

"Don't you know anything?" asked Friendly. "People sing songs about the daring deeds of Robyn-in-the-Hat and the Green Men of Gressingham!"

"I don't get out much," Tom confessed. "I've

never been this far from home before ... and popular songs take ages to reach us."

"Well, you're a brave one, I'll grant you that," said a voice behind him. Tom spun around just as a woman in a big brown hat came out from behind a bush. "As for the rest of you, how can you call yourselves outlaws?" She scowled. "Not one of you spotted me creeping up on you!

I've been listening to every word you've been saying for the past ten minutes. What if I'd been one of Lord Dashwood's spies?"

"But you're not. You're Robyn," said Friendly with a grin. "So no harm be done!"

The other Green Men of Gressingham nodded in agreement.

"So you're Lord Dashwood's nephew, Thomas?" said Robyn-in-the-Hat.

She was dressed like all the outlaws, except for her hat. It was a very strange hat indeed, and Tom could see why it had become part of her name. It was really part hat and part mask. A brown felt flap – yes, it too was brown – came down over the top part of her face. There were two holes, through which Tom could see a pair of sparkling blue eyes, but he doubted that he would recognise Robyn-in-the-Hat without her strange brown hat.

"Why do you disguise yourself when not one of your men does?" asked Tom.

"These men are what they appear to be, Tom," she said. "They're honest to goodness thieves and outlaws. It's the only life they lead. I, on the other hand, lead two lives. For us to be successful, this is ..." She paused to think of the right word. "... necessary."

"I don't know why I should believe a word any of you say about anything," said Tom. "After all those lies about my uncle –"

"Hold your tongue, boy," said Big Jim, with an angry glare. "Outlaws we may be, but we don't lie about Lord Dashwood."

"Cross my heart and hope to die, Tom," said

Friendly. "Dashwood Castle and its lands may once have been a happy place, but not any more."

"Lord Dashwood has made life even harder for the peasants who work on his land, and squeezes taxes from those in the villages. He has appointed a marshal called Guppy to collect the money," said Robyn-in-the-Hat. "Your once-kind uncle has become a cruel and greedy master."

Tom didn't know what to think. What would Robyn and the Green Men of Gressingham have to gain by lying to him?

"The dungeons of Dashwood Castle are now filled with prisoners, most of them innocent people who've tried to stand up to your uncle," she told him.

"But Able Morris said nothing about this," said Tom, nodding in the direction of the still-struggling sack.

"He's not likely to if he's your uncle's man, now is he, Master Tom?" said Robyn.

The conversation was interrupted by another hooting signal. Big Jim clamped his huge hand across Tom's mouth. "Not a word," he whispered.

Fidget lifted a heavy, flat sword from a hiding place behind a rock and pressed the tip of it against Able Morris's sack. "If you don't stop your wriggling and groaning this instant, I'll put an end to you," he hissed through clenched teeth. Able Morris fell silent for the first time since being taken prisoner. Now every Green Man of Gressingham had a weapon in hand and was ready for action.

Chapter 2

A PROMISE TO KEEP

Whoever or whatever Robyn-in-the-Hat and her band of outlaws were expecting, it wasn't a wounded man on a donkey.

"It's Max the Miller!" cried Friendly, rushing forward to help the injured man off his animal. While Friendly and Big Jim carefully lifted the miller down and placed him on the ground, Fidget led the donkey to a bucket of water and let him drink.

"What happened, Max?" asked Robyn, dabbing his head with a piece of cloth. (It was a brown piece of cloth, of course.)

"Lord Dashwood's men came demanding more taxes," groaned the miller. "When I said I had no more money to pay ..." He let out an even bigger groan at the memory of it. "They said they'd take Neddy as payment instead."

"His horse?" gasped Tom. A horse was a very valuable and important thing to anyone in those days, something like a cross between a car and a friend.

"Neddy is his *daughter*," hissed Big Jim. "They have strange names in Max the Miller's family!"

Tom's jaw dropped.

"I tried to stop them ... I tried," said Max.

"I'm sure you did your best," said Robyn. Tom could see tears in her blue eyes through the holes in the mask at the front of her hat.

"There were just too many of them," said the miller. "Too many ..."

"You must rest," said Robyn, patting the wounded man's arm.

"But Neddy!" the miller protested. He tried to sit up but, finding it too painful, lay flat on the ground again.

"Don't you worry," said Robyn. "We will get your Neddy back, safe and well."

Max the Miller looked up at Big Jim, who looked down at him and nodded. "You have the word of Robyn-in-the-Hat, Max," he said. "The deed is as good as done."

At that moment, yet another of the Green

Men arrived. He was dressed as a monk and was clutching a large leather pouch.

"What kept you, Physic?" Robyn demanded. "Max needs the best medicines you have."

"And I need space to work," said Physic. "Give me room."

While Physic looked after his patient, Robyn took Tom by the arm. "Now will you believe us?" she said.

"I–I suppose," said Tom but he still found it difficult to think of his uncle as an evil man.

"This must come as a big surprise to you," said Robyn. "An unhappy one."

"It does," said Tom. All his life, he'd heard such grand stories about his Uncle Alf and how, one day, he'd become one of his knights. Now – on the very day that he had set off for Dashwood

Castle to begin his training – he'd found out that his uncle was feared and hated. "What are you going to do about rescuing the miller's daughter?" he asked.

"Neddy? That rather depends on whether or not you help us," said Robyn, from behind her mask.

"Me?" said Tom. "I thought I was the enemy. How can I help you?"

"The castle lookouts are expecting Able Morris to return with you to the castle," said Robyn. She paused to stir the contents of a cooking pot bubbling over an open fire. "If one ..." she paused and looked at the size of the sack that Able Morris was in, "or two of my Green Men can impersonate Morris, and you are on our side ..."

"Then I can try and free Neddy once I'm inside the castle!"

"Not just Neddy," said Robyn. "We could attack Dashwood Castle and free everyone! We already have a plan to enter the castle, but going through the front door with you could save valuable time. You could be the key to victory that we've been looking for!"

But Robyn's plans made Tom feel a bit sick. "I'd like to help. I really would," he said. "But it seems wrong to betray my uncle. Dashwood Castle has belonged to my family since it was built." He remembered his mother's parting words: *be brave and true.*

"I understand how you feel," said Robyn. "But you saw poor old Max the Miller back there and he's just one of hundreds of people whose lives have been ruined by your uncle's men."

Tom suddenly felt very tired and very confused. "Can I give you my answer in the morning?" he asked.

Robyn-in-the-Hat studied the boy through the eye-holes of her mask. "Do you give me your word as the son of Sir Simon Dashwood that you won't try to escape?"

"I do," said Tom.

"Then you have until morning to decide whether to help us to free Neddy and the others."

Tom nodded.

Later that evening, after Tom had eaten supper as a guest of the Green Men, the outlaws

sang songs around the campfire. It was only a

small fire, so that the light wouldn't be easily

spotted from a distance by the enemy, and they

sang very quietly so as not to be overheard. In

fact, rather than singing around a campfire, it

might be more accurate to describe them as

whispering around a damp fire. Either way, it

was unexciting enough for Tom to find himself

drifting off to sleep surprisingly easily.

He awoke to find himself with someone's hand over his mouth. As his eyes became accustomed to the dark, Tom realised that the hand belonged to Able Morris.

"We must escape from this place," he whispered. "Come!"

Tom groaned. What was he to do now?

Chapter 3

RATHER A PICKLE

Tom looked at Able Morris, who seemed none the worse for wear after all that time in his sack. "I can't," he whispered.

"Can't what?" asked Able.

"Escape."

"Why not, Master Thomas?" asked Able, with a worried frown. "Are you hurt? Have these villains injured you in any way?"

Tom shook his head. "No," he hissed. "It's

just that I've given Robyn-in-the-Hat my word
that I won't try to escape."

"And I've given your uncle, Lord Dashwood,
my solemn oath that I will return with you safely
to Dashwood Castle," said Able Morris, who was,
after all, Lord Dashwood's messenger.

"Oh dear," said Tom. "That leaves us in
rather a pickle then, doesn't it?"

Able nodded in the direction of the edge
of the Green Men's camp and began tiptoeing
away. Tom took that as an order to follow. Out of
earshot of the sleeping outlaws, they continued
their discussion in hushed voices.

"Let me think," said Able. And he thought.

Tom studied the man in the light of early
morning. If only he knew who to trust. Robyn-in-
the-Hat, or Able Morris? Was Able really hiding

the truth from him? Was Uncle Alfred really a ruthless man?

"I have it, Master Thomas!" whispered Able. "I've thought of a way for you to leave this place without you breaking your promise."

"How?" whispered Tom, wide awake now.

"As my prisoner!" grinned Able and, for the second time in twenty-four hours, Tom found himself in a sack. This time with a gag in his mouth.

Many hours later, Tom was let out of the bag. Tom recognised Ferdy at once. Able Morris had managed to steal back his own horse.

Tom lay sprawled on the ground staring up at Ferdy's head framed by the blue sky. "I'm not sure if I should be thanking you or shouting at you!" said Tom, blinking in the bright light of morning.

"This way, I let you keep your honour," said Able, neatly folding the now-empty sack. "You didn't break any promises. I took you away from their camp against your will."

"But they don't know that," Tom protested. He got to his feet. "Where are we?"

"Look behind you," said Able.

So Tom turned and there was Dashwood Castle in all its glory.

He gasped.

It was even more impressive than he'd imagined. It had a high outer wall of thick stone, with a round tower at each corner, surrounded by a moat of dark green water. Soldiers manned the battlements, their highly polished helmets glinting in the morning sun. Tom had seen a picture of the castle in a tapestry and his father had described it to him a thousand times, but nothing had prepared Tom for how he felt now he actually saw this truly magnificent building. This was Dashwood Castle, and he was a Dashwood!

In that moment, Tom felt so proud. Then he remembered everything Robyn-in-the-Hat had said. He thought of Max the Miller. He would ask Uncle Alf about these things as soon as possible.

"Can we go inside?" he asked excitedly.

"That was the whole purpose of our journey," said Able with a smile. He climbed up onto Ferdy and pulled Tom up after him. They rode over the main bridge across the moat, then reached a small tower – called a barbican – where they were met by a guard.

"Halt! Who goes there?" the guard

demanded, waving around a
pike staff rather enthusiastically.

"Able Morris and Master
Thomas Dashwood," said Able. Then
his face broke into a grin. "Let us
through, will you? There's a good
chap."

The guard did not return the smile. "You
may enter," he said and signalled to the main
gate over at the castle. There was a grating
noise and the drawbridge was lowered between
the stretch of moat between the barbican and
the castle. Ferdy completed the last short trot of
Able and Tom's journey.

No sooner had Tom slid off Ferdy and his
feet touched the courtyard floor than a tall, thin,
sandy-haired man in a dark blue cloak appeared

through an archway. "What took you so long?" he demanded.

"We were kidnapped by outlaws, Marshal," said Able, holding his squishy shapeless hat in his hands. He sounded nervous. "But we escaped."

The marshal fixed his stare on Able. "If you say so," he said. "Bring the boy to his uncle. Lord Dashwood is eager to see him and we do so like to keep his lordship happy, don't we?"

"Y–Yes, sire. Always," nodded Able. Ferdy, meanwhile, was being led across the cobbled courtyard to the stable block by one of the many servants who were hard at work inside the castle walls. Tom could hear the drawbridge being winched shut behind them.

"Are you Marshal Guppy?" Tom asked the man in the midnight-blue cloak. Tom had expected him to be bigger and meaner, from the way the outlaws had been talking about him.

"I am," said Marshal Guppy, staring deep into his eyes. "You have heard of me?"

"Yes, sire," said Tom, suddenly feeling very small and unimportant in this huge castle packed with people.

"All good, I hope?" said Marshal Guppy, turning his head away. He laughed a rather nasty laugh. "I'm glad you seem none the worse for your ordeal with the outlaws. Now, go to your uncle!"

*

Lord Dashwood couldn't have been less like Marshal Guppy if he tried. He was a big, round, cheerful man with a huge walrus moustache and every sentence he spoke seemed to contain a chuckle. He was seated on a huge chair and his left leg, bound with bandages, was up on a wooden stool.

"Come, let me take a look at you, Tom!" he said when Able and Tom entered the room. "My brother Simon's baby boy has grown into a fine lad!" He beckoned Tom over and gave him a slap on the back and a hug. "Welcome to Dashwood Castle!"

"Thank you, Uncle," said Tom hurriedly. He had urgent matters to report. "We were taken prisoner by the Green Men of Gressingham! They said that —"

At that very moment, Marshal Guppy strode purposefully into Lord Dashwood's quarters. "Time for your morning medicine, your lordship," he said with rather an over-the-top bow. He handed Tom's uncle a tankard of steaming liquid, which Lord Dashwood drank in one great big gulp.

"Thank you, Guppy," he chuckled. "I don't know what I'd do without you. You're my nursemaid, my adviser, my tax coll ... tax collll ... llll ..." With that, his eyelids fluttered, drooped and well and truly closed.

"You must leave his lordship to sleep now," said the marshal. "He's not a well man. Morris, show the lad his quarters." With that, he picked up the empty tankard and swept out of the room.

"My uncle's not well? Why didn't you tell me this, Able?" Tom demanded.

"Orders," said Able. "Lord Dashwood doesn't want people thinking he's weak. They look to him to protect them and make important decisions for them. He is responsible for the lives of all the peasants for miles around ..."

"What's wrong with him?" asked Tom.

"He hurt his foot in a riding accident, when he was thrown from his horse. Since then he has never fully regained his strength and spends his days here inside his quarters. The medicine often makes him drowsy. Sometimes he sleeps right through the day. I spend my time here with him. That's why he needs Marshal Guppy to run things for him, to do his bidding."

"Or to do his own bidding," Tom muttered.

"What do you mean?" demanded Able, opening a chest and removing a large blanket which he proceeded to put over his sleeping master.

"Well, it seems like Guppy gets a free hand to do what he likes, in my uncle's name ... and if the people don't like it, my uncle gets the blame."

"But that's ridiculous, Master Thomas!" Able protested. "I mean, I would know if there were strange things afoot, would I not?"

"Would you? Didn't you say you spend all your time in here with Uncle Alf? You've no idea what's going on out in the villages or down in the dungeons, have you?"

"Well ... er ... Why would the marshal risk sending me out into the world to bring you here, in case I saw something that I shouldn't? He could have sent one of the guards." Able Morris opened a wooden shutter and sunlight streamed through a glassless window into Lord Dashwood's quarters.

"Was it Marshal Guppy or Uncle Alf who asked you to collect me?" asked Tom, peering out of the window to the moat below. The long drop made him feel a bit queasy.

"Your uncle ..."

"And, if Marshal Guppy wants him to think that everything is fine, he can't openly go against his wishes, can he? So of course you had to be the one to collect me," Tom argued.

Able Morris sat in a chair by his now-snoring master. "I simply don't know what to think," he sighed.

"If only I could get to the dungeons to see if Max the Miller's daughter, Neddy, is being held prisoner in there," said Tom. "That would soon tell us who is telling the truth."

Just then, there was a scuttling sound and Tom caught a glimpse of a shadow moving in the corridor. "Someone was listening at the doorway!" he cried. "They'll probably report back to Guppy and then we're done for!"

Both Able and Tom hurried to the doorway. "Then we must act quickly," said Able. "Let's look in the dungeons and, if you're right, we'll tell your uncle everything when he wakes up. Follow me!"

Chapter 4

A PLAN OF ATTACK

Able Morris may have been a little on the large side – actually, he was a lot on the large size – but Tom had trouble keeping up with him as they dashed through a maze of corridors and stone stairways. Tom knew that he'd never be able to find his way back on his own. They were going deeper and deeper into the castle.

"What if they won't let us in the dungeon?" Tom panted.

"Then you must try to find a way to have a peek inside while I distract the guard, Master Thomas," said Able.

Tom rounded a corner to find they had arrived. Able Morris kept in front of him. "Lord Dashwood has bid me inspect the dungeon," Able told a rather dopey-looking guard who was in need of a shave.

"Let me see your orders," said the guard.

"I don't have written orders," said Able, trying to sound as indignant and haughty as he could. "I am Able Morris, his lordship's personal aide, not a common soldier who needs written orders ..."

"Well, I am a common soldier who does need written orders, sire, and I'm not going to risk my neck by letting you past without ..."

While the two men argued, Tom slipped behind the guard's back and, keeping to the shadows, made his way down the corridor. At the end, instead of a stone wall, was a heavy wooden door. There were two small windows level with Tom's ankles and an iron grille on either side of the door. Through the grille, Tom could see down to a gloomy room below, with a straw-covered floor. It was full of prisoners. Hundreds of them. Some chained. Some free to move about. Men, women and children. Young and old. The one thing they all had in common was that they looked thin and very dirty. Tom's heart sank. This was a very sorry sight.

Tom pressed his face up against the grille. "Pssssssssssst!" he said. "Pssssssssssssssst!"

"Who is it?" called one of the prisoners.

"Ssssh!" Tom hushed frantically. "Is Neddy the miller's daughter there?" he whispered.

There was some movement and, eventually, a small blond girl with tear-stained cheeks was lifted up to the grille. She clutched the bars and peered through them at Tom. "What is it?" she whispered. "Is my father all right? Who are you?"

"I'm a friend," whispered Tom. "Your father is fine. His wounds were tended to by Physic, one of the Green Men of Gressingham. The Green Men are making plans to rescue you all. Be brave. Tell the others that help will come. Robyn-in-the-Hat is on her way."

The poor girl squealed with excitement. Tom heard the murmuring at the end of the corridor stop suddenly, and saw the guard running in his direction. There was nowhere to hide. Instead of trying to dodge him, Tom dashed straight at him and then, at the very last moment, dived between his legs. This sent the guard toppling to the stone floor with a nasty crunch as Tom and Able made a hasty retreat.

"Ooooooooh! I've got a nosebleed!" the guard wailed as Tom followed Able down the seemingly endless passageways.

They eventually found themselves in a room with a large built-in oak wardrobe along one wall. In fact, the whole room was called the wardrobe. Able checked to see they were alone. They seemed to be. "Well?" he asked.

"The miller's daughter was there, Able," said Tom. "I believe Robyn-in-the-Hat and everything she said. I know it's difficult for you to believe, because you and my uncle have been tricked, but I think Dashwood Castle has turned bad and it's the outlaws who are on the side of good now!"

"If you are correct, Master Thomas, once the eavesdropper reports to Guppy what he overheard, and then the dungeon guard does the same, it'll be too late for us to do anything," said a stunned Able. "Guppy will lock us up too, and then come up with some reason for our absence that will satisfy your uncle –"

"Which shouldn't be too difficult since the old fool spends much of his life drugged up to the eyeballs with my sleeping draughts," sneered Marshal Guppy, stepping out of the oak wardrobe.

Tom was stunned. How was he to know that
the wardrobe was just one of the many entrances
and exits to the castle's secret passages?

"I think I'll arrange a jousting accident,"
said Guppy. "Poor little Tom was eager to have
his first joust and silly old Able Morris eager to

arrange one, with tragic consequences. I imagine there will be a lot of blood and broken bones ... Take them away."

Two soldiers stepped out of the wardrobe behind Guppy and grabbed Able and Tom roughly, pointing the sharp tips of their swords into their backs.

*

One of the most important things a castle needs is often overlooked today. We all think of the portcullis, the thick doors, the easily defended battlements, the moat and – the brainier among us – the castle's defensive position in the landscape, on high ground looking down. What we often forget is the well – the water supply. Without water, the occupants would have died of thirst.

Dashwood Castle had a large well housed in its own room on the ground floor. The water was fairly clear by medieval standards, but you'd still be glad to drink beer instead, even first thing in the morning. That particular Sunday morning, however, something very strange was going on in the well room. Every few minutes a head would appear at the top of the well and a naked man would climb out. Each man was carrying a weapon and a small waterproof sack. From out of the sack, he brought a dry, brown monk's habit which he slipped on and then concealed his weapon inside.

The men were all different shapes and sizes. One was huge. One was round. One was fidgety. One was very squat. And the others were everything in between. Soon the room was packed with these hooded monks – though it's doubtful that they were really there for Morning Mass. When all that were going to clamber out of the well had clambered out of the well, the monks drifted into the castle courtyard.

The first Tom learned about their presence was when a friendly face appeared at the high window in his single cell. The friendly face belonged to Friendly, the jolliest of the Green Men of Gressingham. "Fear not, Tom, help is at hand!" he whispered.

"I thought you thought I was the enemy!" cried Tom.

"Never!" Friendly beamed. "You told the others help was on the way ... You're a prisoner in your uncle's own castle. That makes you a friend, Master Tom." He threw one end of a knotted rope down to him.

Tom had climbed up that rope and squeezed through the bars of his cell before you could say "Down with Guppy!" He found himself in some deserted inner, inner courtyard.

"What about the others?" Tom asked.

"Big Jim has freed the prisoners from the main dungeon, and your friend Able Morris was among them," said Friendly, coiling up the rope and hiding it inside his monk's habit. "If we're caught, we're only outnumbered by 500 to 1, so we should be fine. We fight best when the odds are against us."

"But if we can get to my uncle and tell him what's been going on, then we may be able to turn the odds in our favour," said Tom.

Friendly frowned. "I don't know if us Green Men have ever taken on a mission with the odds in our favour. Now there's a novel idea!"

"If only I knew my way around the castle," Tom groaned. "I haven't the foggiest idea where Uncle Alf's chambers are."

"Have no fear!" said Friendly. "I have a map ..." He put his hand up one sleeve. Nothing. "Somewhere ..." he said, pulling a rolled up map out of the other. "Now, let's see."

Chapter 5

A FINAL FIGHT

Lord Dashwood was very surprised to be awoken by his nephew and a jolly-looking monk. "Good morning, young Tom. What's going on?"

"You've been tricked, Uncle Alf," Tom explained. "Since you injured your foot and haven't been able to get around your castle and lands, Marshal Guppy has been doing terrible things in your name. He's been overworking the peasants, over taxing the villagers and probably pocketing the money for himself. He's even been imprisoning innocent people here in the castle. I saw them with my own eyes last night. Women and children."

Lord Dashwood looked at Friendly in horror. "Is this true?" he asked, struggling to sit up.

"It is, my lord," said Friendly, "though, sadly, I thought these wrongdoings were on your orders until the boy put me straight ..."

"In my name?" gasped Lord Dashwood. "I must act to put things right!" He looked around the room. "Where is Able Morris? Is he one of Marshal Guppy's men, or still loyal to me?"

"He's most loyal, Uncle –" said Tom.

"You don't know how much it gladdens me to hear that," said Lord Dashwood.

"– But he was taken prisoner too," said Tom. He quickly told his uncle everything that had happened since Able Morris had collected him from the manor house and what they had discovered. As Tom talked, he and Friendly helped to dress Lord Dashwood in his finest armour (which wasn't easy with his lordship hopping around on one leg).

"So the Green Men are already here now, setting prisoners free," said Lord Dashwood. "This is an excellent time to strike back ... Tom, you will be my walking stick. I will lean on you. Enough talk. Now to action!"

Many of the guards and servants who saw his lordship, flanked by Tom and a jolly monk, were surprised to see their master up and about – but pleased too. They bowed and curtseyed as he made his way outside.

In the courtyard, they were greeted by an extraordinary sight: a group of monks and freed prisoners – many of them in rags – in arm-to-arm combat with the castle guards. With the hoods of their monks' habits now thrown back, it was easy to recognise which Green Man was which, and they all seemed to be thoroughly enjoying a good punch-up. Fists, arrows and rocks were flying everywhere.

As Tom arrived on the scene, Big Jim was picking up a soldier in each hand and banging their heads together with a satisfying THUNK. The element of surprise and the attack from within meant that everything seemed to be going the outlaws' way, until the tide suddenly turned. Into the courtyard clattered Marshal Guppy and a group of heavily armed knights.

"Kill them all!" cried Guppy, drawing his sword, and the knights drew theirs too.

"WAIT!" boomed a voice, ringing with authority.

The knights hesitated. It was a voice they knew well but had not heard in a long time. It belonged to their lord and master. Helped by Tom, Lord Dashwood hobbled forward and stood on the stone steps to the chapel, head and shoulders above the crowd.

"STOP FIGHTING!" he bellowed. The effect was impressive. Even the outlaws and freed prisoners stopped to see what was happening.

"There will be no killing here today!"

Lord Dashwood proclaimed. "Though someone may soon hang for the bad deeds he's done in my name."

"The old fool's rambling," cried Marshal Guppy. "Why do you think I've been put in charge? He's losing his mind ..."

"I am your master, not he!" Lord Dashwood reminded them, looking every inch a baron and ruler in his gleaming armour, Tom standing proudly at his side on the chapel steps.

Guppy had misjudged badly. Being a knight was a job based on chivalry and honour to one's lord, even if you didn't always like what he asked of you. Many of the knights had been unhappy at the orders Guppy had given them but, genuinely believing them to be from Lord Dashwood, they had carried them out. Now it was clear that

Guppy had been acting on his own ...

Marshal Guppy could see that his run of good luck was over. "Come, Sir Clarence!" he said to the one evil knight who'd been in on his nasty plan from the outset. "Time to move on!" With a dig of his spurs, he galloped his horse towards the gatehouse. "Lower the drawbridge!" he screamed.

Unaware of what had been happening elsewhere, the guards in the gatehouse followed the marshal's orders.

"He's getting away!" cried Tom.

"Don't be so sure of that, Master Tom!" laughed Big Jim. He then turned his attention to a couple of soldiers lying on the cobbled ground, lifting them up and dusting them down. "No hard feelings, ay?" he said.

Everyone swarmed to the drawbridge in time to see Guppy and Sir Clarence gallop half way across, only to be confronted by a lone figure – on foot – barring their exit. It was Robyn-in-the-Hat herself!

"ROBYN! ROBYN!" cheered the Green Men.

With a brief bow to her onlookers and a skilful twirl of her staff, she knocked Guppy clean off his horse. The marshal flew in a graceful arc through the air and into the inky green moat, where he sank below the surface like a sack of stones.

The cheers of the crowd – made up of outlaws, freed prisoners and Dashwood's loyal men – drowned out the second SPLASH as Sir Clarence joined his scheming master in the moat. A moment later, he bobbed to the surface,

spluttering and choking in the foul water.

"Where's Guppy?" asked Tom, running onto the drawbridge and looking into the moat. "He's not getting away underwater, is he?"

Without so much as a word, Robyn-in-the-Hat dived in and disappeared from view. After an agonising wait, she surfaced with her sodden felt mask flat against her face. She was holding Guppy. A dozen pairs of arms pulled them to safety.

"He weighs a ton!" she gasped and, tearing at his cloak, soon discovered why. Gold coins tumbled out of the soaked material onto the wood of the drawbridge. "His cloak has gold sewn into its lining!" Robyn laughed. This secret hoard, designed for an emergency getaway, had almost been the death of him.

Helped by Friendly, Lord Dashwood walked onto the bridge. At that moment, Able Morris ran from the group of freed prisoners that he'd been fighting alongside, and stood by his master and Tom.

"Hello, my loyal friend," beamed his lordship. "Glad to see you're unharmed." The two men hugged. Then Lord Dashwood turned to Robyn. "I have much to thank you for," he said.

"But we have much to apologise for, in turn, your lordship," said Robyn-in-the-Hat. "If it weren't for your nephew Thomas here, we'd still believe that you were behind all this cruelty and wrongdoing. We should have known that you are and always have been a good man."

"A good man fooled by a bad one," said Tom.

"But all's well that ends well," said Lord Dashwood, putting a hand on Tom's shoulder.

*

Two nights later there were celebrations in the great hall of the castle. Lord Dashwood had sent out messengers to invite people from many miles around to attend a mighty banquet. There was music and dancing and juggling as well as much feasting. Of course, Tom's parents were there and, of course his mother was crying, but for joy this time. His father was looking very proud of what Tom had done.

People who hadn't seen Lord Dashwood for months were delighted to find him his old self. They had heard rumours of a terrible illness and had been upset and frightened by how he seemed to rule his lands with an iron fist. Now they knew that the iron fist, Guppy, had been working alone. Lord Dashwood was his old, kind, chuckling self. Physic had taken a look at his leg wound and his treatment had already worked wonders.

As for the guests of honour, they were

none other than the Green Men of Gressingham, seated in pride of place at the high table. Tom sat next to Squat who was sitting on a pile of cushions so that he could see over the table top. But the Green Men's leader, Robyn, was nowhere to be seen.

"Who are you looking for?" asked a voice.

Tom turned in his seat. There, sitting to his right at the table laden with food, was a beautiful young woman, dressed in a long green robe of the latest of fashions. "Robyn-in-the-Hat, my lady," he explained.

"You have met this leader of outlaws?" she asked. "She sounds most exciting."

"She is," said Tom. "Her Green Men kidnapped me, but we soon became friends."

"Is she beautiful?" asked the lady, with a

strange smile on her lips.

"I've never seen her face," Tom confessed. He looked at his questioner. Her eyes were a sparkling blue.

They were interrupted by Tom's Uncle Alf banging his flagon on the table. "A toast!" he cried, rising to his feet. Everyone in the great hall of Dashwood Castle stood up as one. "To the Green Men of Gressingham," he said.

They all raised their goblets and tankards. "The Green Men of Gressingham!" they cried.

The lady with the sparkling blue eyes winked at Tom.

Could she have been? No, surely not ... but then again, she might have been, mighten she?

FROM THE D[ESK OF]

ADRIAN [DONGLE]

Sir Philip

You've been saying you've been wanting to write another Green Men of Gressingham story.
Now's your chance!

Dotty

Dear Mrs Hendrix

Although this letter is 'FROM THE DESK OF ADRIAN DONGLE' I am not, in fact, Adrian but his brother, David Dongle. Please call me 'Dave'.

Sadly, Adrian had an accident with a garden hosepipe, but the last thing he shouted as they took him away in the ambulance was "Please get Philip Ardagh to write another book about the Green Men of Gressingham!" He loved the first story SO much.

Could we arrange a meeting between myself and Sir Philip to discuss this?

It would be wonderful to be able to bring good news to my brother Adrian in his hospital bed.

Very best wishes

D.Dongle

Dave Dongle
Publisher

D, Don't tell this Dave Dongle person that. Tell him that we have important matters to discuss over a large lunch. (Come up with a few 'worries' I might have, will you? Thank you.) I'd like to try that new restaurant THE HAPPY PUDDING. See if you can fix that up, will you? Thanks, P.A.

AH

⚘ ARDAGH HOUSE ⚘

Dear Mr Dongle

Please forgive my not calling you 'Dave', but I hardly know you.

Sir Philip is certainly interested in the idea of writing a brand new Green Men of Gressingham adventure but, as well as being VERY busy, he does have a few worries:

1. The Green Men of Gressingham are no longer outlaws.

2. The evil Marshal Guppy has been defeated.

3. Robyn-in-the-Hat, Big Jim and the others are now all friends of Lord Dashwood of Dashwood Castle.

So what on earth could they all get up to in a new story?

Sir Philip has a meeting up in town on Thursday morning next week and was wondering whether he could meet you at a nearby restaurant for lunch afterwards. How about The Happy Pudding?

I look forward to hearing from you.

Yours sincerely

Dotty Hendrix

Dotty Hendrix (Mrs)

P.S. I do hope that your brother Adrian is recovering from his accident with the hosepipe.

Sir Philip Ardagh
Ardagh House
Hillington-on-the-w

Sir Philip

You've got your lunch at
The Happy Pudding.

All systems go!

D

Dear Mrs Hendrix

I have ordered some new headed letter paper with 'Dave Dongle' on it, but it hasn't arrived yet. I am THRILLED that Sir Philip likes the idea of writing a new Green Men adventure.

I'm sure that a writer of his extraordinary talent will have no trouble getting over the 'worries' you mentioned in your letter.

Next Thursday will be fine. I have booked a table at The Happy Pudding for one o'clock and have let the restaurant know that we may be there some time. (My brother once mentioned how Sir Philip likes to try most things on a menu.)

I look forward to seeing Sir Philip then.

Very best wishes

D. Dongle

Dave Dongle
Publisher

D, I like this Dave Dongle. He knows a good writer when he reads one. Good news about the lunch too AND I'm buzzing with ideas for the new Gressingham story.

I'm thinking DRAGONS. P.A.

THE HAPPY BANANAS
OF GRESSINGHAM

Dragon Quest

MUSHROOMS!

Smells of mushrooms!

Tom
goes
too...

The
Happy
Pudding
Menu

THE GREEN DRAGONS OF GRESSINGHAM???

~~THE DRAGONS OF GRESSINGHAM~~

I ♥
CHEESE
CAKE

THE RED DRAGONS
OF GRESSINGHAM ✓

The Pig!

The Pig!

Dotty, Had a fabulous lunch and meeting. Jotted down a few ideas as we ate. Please turn them into a letter to Dave.

Thanks, P.A.

P.S. We've run out of bananas again.

ARDAGH HOUSE

Dear Mr Dongle

Sir Philip tells me that your lunchtime meeting was a great success and that he's DELIGHTED to write a second Gressingham adventure.

It will involve the Green Men, Tom and a dragon quest, and it will be called THE RED DRAGONS OF GRESSINGHAM.

The outlaws' pig will also put in another appearance.

He'll be starting work right away.

Yours sincerely

Dotty Hendrix

Dotty Hendrix (Mrs)

P.S. How is your brother Adrian?

DD FROM THE DESK OF
DAVE DONGLE

Dear Mrs Hendrix

That's FANTASTIC news. I can't wait to read the new adventure.

Another piece of good news is that my new headed letter paper has arrived. Like it?

And, while I remember, please tell Sir Philip not to worry and that I managed to get the tomato sauce stains out of my trousers.

Very best wishes

D. Dongle

Dave Dongle
Publisher

P.S. Adrian was supposed to leave hospital yesterday but tripped over a nurse and is back in bed.

AH

❧ ARDAGH HOUSE ❧

Dear Dave,

Here it is. THE RED DRAGONS OF
GRESSINGHAM.

ENJOY!

Philip Ardagh

P.S. We must have lunch together again
soon.

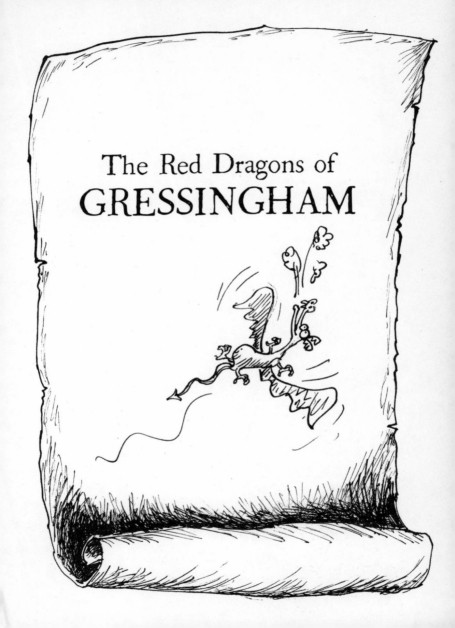

The Red Dragons of
GRESSINGHAM

When Gressingham was ruled by the evil Marshal Guppy, the Green Men were a busy band of outlaws. Now that Lord Dashwood is back in charge at the castle, the Green Men of Gressingham have no one to fight and nothing to do ... until his lordship comes up with a plan. He will send the Green Men on a special quest. A special quest where all is perhaps not quite as it seems.

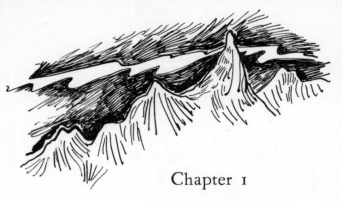

Chapter 1

OLD FRIENDS

Big Jim was bored. Fidget was bored. Friendly was bored. In fact, all of the Green Men of Gressingham were bored. They were hanging around the forest, yawning.

Fidget was fidgeting. Friendly was trying to make friends with an ant, and Big Jim was leaning against a tree. Big Jim was big, but the tree was even bigger. Much bigger. This used to be their lookout tree: the one they climbed up to be on the lookout for their enemies, in the days when they were outlaws. Now they didn't have any enemies to look out for. It was now their drying tree. They hung their washing on the tree instead.

Physic was the roundest of all the Green Men. He was busy hanging clothes on the branches to dry. They were all brown. As you know, this was because the Green Men all wore brown. Brown hid the dirt better than green, and they didn't wash their clothes that often.

"I'm so bored," said Physic hanging the last brown sock on the tree.

"Me too," said Big Jim. "I wish some bandits would come into the forest and we could have a good old punch-up."

"We haven't had a fight for ages and ages," said Fidget.

"And ages and ages and ages," added Friendly, who was the one Green Man who didn't like fighting much anyway.

"Why don't we have a bow and arrow contest?" suggested Lanky. Lanky was almost as tall as Big Jim but he was very, very, very thin.

"We did that yesterday," Friendly said with a yawn.

"How about a pie-eating contest?" said Physic.

The other Green Men stared at Physic's great big tummy. "We did that the day before yesterday," said Big Jim.

"And you always win!" said Squat. "It's not much of a contest."

Physic grinned. "I do, don't I?" he said.

Physic loved pies.

"We could tidy the camp?" Friendly suggested. He had given up on the ant and was now being friendly to a buttercup.

"Oh, for goodness' sake," shouted Big Jim. "We are outlaws! Outlaws don't do housework!"

"We're not outlaws any more," Friendly reminded him. "Now we're in-laws. We are on the same side as the law now that the evil Marshal Guppy is behind bars."

Big Jim frowned. "That's true," he said at last. "But I still don't like housework."

"Hard luck," said Physic, "because it's your turn to feed Martha."

Martha was the Green Men's pet pig. She was very big and very pink. It was hard to tell that she was pink because she loved to roll in the mud. She always looked as brown as the Green Men's clothes.

Big Jim muttered something under his breath. He picked up a bucket of acorns and went over to the pig pen. He didn't mind really. He was very fond of Martha and feeding her gave him something to do.

The pig pen was empty.

"Martha has gone!" he shouted.

"Gone?" shouted the others.

"Gone!" shouted Big Jim.

The others rushed over to see what he was talking about. Big Jim was right. Martha, the mud-covered pig, was nowhere to be seen.

"How did Martha get out?" Friendly wondered. "The gate to the pig pen is still closed."

"She's been stolen!" said Physic. He looked very upset. He loved Martha. He even ate like her.

"You were hoping for bandits in the forest, Big Jim," said Lanky.

"And now we've got at least one," said Fidget. "A bandit who is also a pig thief!"

Squat, the smallest of all the Green Men, picked up a sword and waved it above his head. This wasn't hard because most things were above his head anyway. It was a very large sword. "We must find the thief and get Martha back!" he shouted.

At that moment, something stung Squat's neck. He dropped the sword in surprise. It stuck in the ground like the sword that King Arthur had to pull from the stone. "Ouch!" he said.

"What's wrong?" asked Big Jim.
Then something stung him on the
cheek. "Ouch!" he shouted.

"What the –?" began Friendly, but he
got no further. Now something stung him on the
forehead.

"Shhh!" said Fidget. He pointed to a clump
of bushes.

The Green Men stopped and listened. Big
Jim pulled the sword out of the ground. Lanky
picked up his bow and pulled out an arrow from
the quiver on his back. Physic grabbed his staff
(which was really just a very long stick). Squat
picked up what he thought was a stone but
turned out to be a sleeping hedgehog. He put it
down very quickly.

The Green Men could hear sounds coming

from the bushes. They sounded like someone trying very hard not to laugh.

"COME ON OUT!" shouted Big Jim. "We've got you surrounded."

A head popped out above the top of the leaves. It was Tom Dashwood, Lord Dashwood's nephew! It was Tom who had helped the Green Men free Lord Dashwood from the evil clutches of Marshal Guppy, and bring peace back to Gressingham.

Tom was grinning from ear to ear. "Hello, everyone," he said. He came out of his hiding place. In one hand he was holding a piece of rope. In the other he was holding a hollow reed he'd been using like a pea-shooter. The Green Men put down their weapons.

"So that's what the stinging was!" Big Jim

laughed. "You were shooting dried peas at us."

"What a waste." Physic sighed. "Those dried peas would make a nice soup."

Now Tom laughed. "Trust you to be thinking of your tummy," he said. He tugged the rope and Martha came out from behind the bush.

"Oink!" grunted Martha.

"Call yourself a bunch of outlaws?" said Tom, still smiling. "I stole Martha from right under your noses."

"Strictly speaking, we're not outlaws any more," Friendly reminded him with a grin.

"Anyway, Martha would have squealed if you were a stranger," said Big Jim.

The Green Men were pleased to see Tom. Now that he was busy training to be a knight at the castle, they didn't see him very often. They sat around the campfire and asked him for any news. Physic put on a pot of water to boil to make some nettle tea.

"How are things at Dashwood Castle?" asked Friendly.

"How is your training going?" asked Squat. "Will you be a knight soon?"

"No." Tom put his head in his hands and sighed. "I'm beginning to think I'll be a page boy for ever." Then his face brightened. He smiled. "But I have good news for you. My uncle, Lord Dashwood, has summoned you all to Dashwood Castle!"

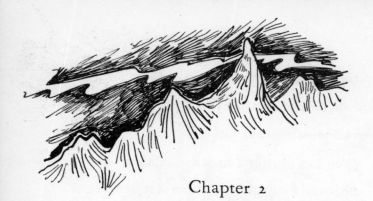

Chapter 2

THE UNEXPLAINED AND UNEXPLAINABLE

The Green Men of Gressingham set off for the castle at once. That night they slept at the Swan Inn, under the sign of a blue bull. (Don't ask.) The following morning, the in-laws continued their journey to the castle. They were met by a woman riding a beautiful jet-black horse.

"Robyn!" called out a delighted Tom Dashwood. It was Robyn-in-the-Hat, leader of

the Green Men. Tom rode up

alongside her. "It's good to

see you again," he said.

"You too, Master Tom," she replied.

She was called Robyn-in-the-Hat because of

the strange hat she wore. It was half hat and half

mask. A felt flap came down over the top part

of her face. There were two holes through which

you could see her sparkling blue eyes.

Robyn used to wear the hat to hide her

true identity. Now that the Green Men were no

longer outlaws, many people expected her to

stop wearing it, but she didn't. "The secret must

remain," she had said.

"Do you know what your uncle, Lord

Dashwood, wants with you all?" she asked Tom.

"Is Gressingham in danger again?"

"No danger," said Tom. "He said he has a surprise for you."

"And you don't know what it is?"

Tom shook his head. "It will be a surprise for me, too."

"I don't like surprises," said Fidget, who was trotting on his horse directly behind them.

They reached Dashwood Castle many hours later. The sentry on lookout duty on the battlements of the castle gatehouse saw the Green Men long before they reached the gate. By the time they arrived, a small crowd had gathered to greet them. Tom's friend Able Morris stood at the front. He was wearing his favourite squishy hat.

"Greetings, Master Thomas!" he said. "I see you found our fearless friends."

"Yes," said Tom as he jumped down from his horse. "And they are as eager as I am to find out what my uncle wants them for."

"They will find out soon enough," said Able. "You are all to go to the great hall at once."

Just as soon as their horses had been settled in the castle stables, Tom led Robyn-in-the-Hat and the Green Men to the great hall. Tom's uncle, Lord Dashwood, was sitting in a big wooden chair at the far end. He stood up when they came in.

"Welcome," he said. "I've been waiting for you."

*

After the formal greetings were over, Lord Dashwood explained why he had summoned Robyn and the Green Men to the castle. "I want you to go to the Red Rock Mountains," he said. "You too, Tom."

Tom was amazed. "But no one goes to the Red Rock Mountains, Uncle Alf!" he said. The mountains were famous for being wild and unexplored.

"Not if they can help it," muttered Fidget.

"We'll need to take plenty of supplies, your lordship!" said Physic, already planning some menus in his head.

"It could be – er – dangerous, sire," Friendly added.

"I thought you liked danger," said Lord Dashwood.

"Like it? We thrive on it, my lord," said Robyn-in-the-Hat. Tom could see her eyes sparkling with excitement.

"There's just the small matter of the dragons," said Squat.

"Who said that?" asked Lord Dashwood. He leaned forward in his throne-like chair.

Squat stepped out of Big Jim's big shadow. "Me, your lordship."

"And you think dragons are just a small matter?" asked Lord Dashwood. He looked around the great hall at all the other Green Men. "If the smallest man among you thinks dragons are just a small matter, then I know I've chosen the right people!"

Squat wanted to point out that he was only joking. He considered dragons to be a very BIG problem indeed. He wanted to say that one of the last things on Earth he wanted to do was meet a dragon. In fact, if he were to meet a dragon it would probably be the last thing he did on Earth, because the scaly beast would either eat him or roast him alive with its fiery breath.

"Chosen us for what, Uncle?" asked Tom.

"For a quest, of course," said Lord Dashwood. "I want you to go to the Red Rock Mountains and bring me back a dragon."

Now it wasn't just Tom Dashwood who was amazed. Everyone was, except for Lord Dashwood, of course. He was busy grinning behind his great big walrus moustache.

"A dragon quest," said Robyn-in-the-Hat. "It will be an honour, my lord."

"But what do you need a dragon for?" asked Friendly.

"Forgive the men, my lord," said Robyn. Tom guessed that she was frowning hard at Friendly from behind her mask. "We relish the challenge of bringing you back a dragon."

"You did say *dragon*, didn't you, my lord?" asked Fidget. "One of those giant, scaly, fire-breathing monsters?"

"The very same," said Lord Dashwood with a nod.

"But don't they eat people?" asked Friendly. "I'm sure I heard somewhere that they eat people."

"Baron Hankey tells me that he has one over in Woolton," said Lord Dashwood. "He didn't say anything about it eating anybody."

"Maybe that's not something people like to talk about, sire," muttered Squat.

"When do we start, your lordship?" asked Big Jim. Anything was better than sitting around twiddling his thumbs.

"After a large meal?" Physic suggested.

The great hall echoed with Lord Dashwood's booming laughter. "What an excellent idea!" he said.

*

After a very fine meal, the Green Men made plans for their quest. There were no maps of the Red Rock Mountains themselves. This was because so few people had been there. Or because those who had gone there had never come back. However, there were maps showing the best ways to reach the mountains. The tables had been cleared and the maps laid on them.

"What's that squiggle?" Friendly pointed.

"I think it's a stream," said Able Morris. He

took a closer look at the map.

"And that big round thing?" asked Friendly.

"I think that's supposed to be a big boulder," said Able Morris.

"And that thing which looks like a squashed fly?"

Tom Dashwood leaned in very close. He scratched the mark on the map that Friendly was now pointing at. "It is a squashed fly," he said.

"This map reading business is easy!" Friendly laughed.

"That may be so," said Lord Dashwood, "but I have asked a dragon expert to accompany you on your quest. His name is Dredwich." He turned to Able Morris and spoke in his ear.

Able nodded his head and hurried out of

the great hall. His squishy hat bobbed on top of his head as he walked. He returned moments later with a man dressed in a dark, hooded robe. The man smelled strongly of damp fungus: earthy toadstools and soggy mushrooms.

He bowed before Lord Dashwood of Dashwood Castle, who introduced him to the others. "This is Dredwich," he announced.

"An honour to meet the Green Men of Gressingham," said Dredwich. "It is thanks to you that the evil Marshal Guppy is now in the dungeon where he belongs. I am your humble servant and adviser for this dangerous quest."

Big Jim slapped the man on the back. "If you know anything about dragons then you know more about dragons than the rest of us put together," he boomed.

"Except for the eating people part," said Friendly.

"And the big and scaly fire-eating part," said Squat.

"It would seem you know more about dragons than you think," said Dredwich. He gave a wheezy cough.

"Are you a professional dragon expert?" asked Tom, who wasn't put off by the man's strange smell of damp fungus.

"I am master of the unexplained and unexplainable," Dredwich wheezed.

"What do you mean by that, sire?" asked Tom.

"I can't explain," said Dredwich. He cleared his throat. "Now, I must make preparations for the dragon quest." He bowed to Lord Dashwood again. "Good day, your lordship." He then bowed to Robyn-in-the-Hat. "Madam," he said then, turning to the others, said, "Good day to you all." He left the great hall leaving a trail of a light dusting of soil behind him

"An odd fellow," said Big Jim.

"He smelled of old mushrooms," said Friendly.

"I like mushrooms," said Physic, which came as no surprise to anyone.

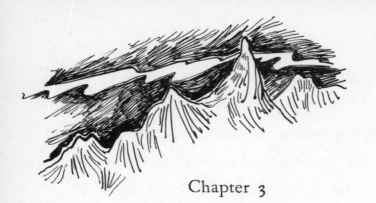

Chapter 3

MR NUZZLE AND
STUBBORN THE MULE

Tom found it hard to sleep that night. A
dragon quest! What could be more exciting?
His tummy felt very funny indeed. It was
churning with a mixture of excitement and fear.
Most of the others felt the same at breakfast.
Very few of the Green Men ate more than a few
mouthfuls, except for Big Jim.

The reason why Physic didn't eat anything

was because he wasn't there.
(If he had been there, I'm sure
he would have eaten plenty.) He had got up long
before the others and gone down to the castle
kitchens. There, he had made friends with the
castle's cook. By the time breakfast came around,
he had gathered plenty of supplies for the quest.
There were lots of sacks and barrels. All Physic
had to do now was to find a way of carrying
them all.

He tracked down Tom after breakfast. "Will
Lord Dashwood lend us extra horses to carry our
supplies?" he asked.

"I'm sure he will," Tom said with a nod.
"After all, this is his *special* quest we're going on,
remember? I'll speak to Able about it."

Tom spoke to Able and Able spoke to Mr

Nuzzle, who was in charge of the castle's stables. This was a very important job. One of the things that set knights apart from foot soldiers was that knights rode horses. (Foot soldiers went on foot!) A knight couldn't be a proper knight without a horse, so horses needed looking after. That's what Mr Nuzzle did. He even looked like a horse. Perhaps that's why the animals liked him.

Able Morris told Mr Nuzzle about the Green Men's need for more horses.

"There is one slight problem, sire," said Mr Nuzzle. "With the celebrations coming up, and Sir Flayling's horse lame, we only have two spare."

"Very well," said Able Morris. "We'll take the two spare ones, please."

"But I could also offer them Stubborn."

"Stubborn?" asked Able.

"Stubborn," nodded Mr Nuzzle.

"Isn't Stubborn a mule?" Able asked.

Mr Nuzzle nodded again.

"A very stubborn mule?" asked Able.

"Yes, sire," said Mr Nuzzle. "Hence the name."

"Hence the name," Able muttered.

A mule has a donkey for a father and a horse for a mother. There is a saying "as stubborn as a mule". Can you guess why that is? Yes, you're right. Mules can be very stubborn. They only do something if they *want* to do it. For a mule to be actually given the name Stubborn must mean that it was a very stubborn mule indeed.

"Stubborn will have to do," Able sighed.

"Please get her and the two horses ready."

"Right away, sire," said Mr Nuzzle. He called for the nearest stable boy, who came scurrying out of the straw.

*

Lord Dashwood was in his private chamber. He had a single visitor.

"You are clear on your duties?" he asked the hooded figure of Dredwich.

"Yes, your lordship. To keep Robyn-in-the-Hat and the others away from the castle for as long as possible."

"Exactly!" said Lord Dashwood. "I don't care what lies you tell them or what false trails you lead them on, but you must keep them away from here at all costs. Is that understood?"

"Perfectly, your lordship. Perfectly."

"Good. Good luck."

"Thank you, your lordship." Dredwich opened the door and walked out into the corridor, leaving a fresh trail of old soil behind him.

*

Many members of the castle household came out to cheer off Robyn-in-the Hat, the Green Men, Tom Dashwood and Dredwich. It wasn't every day that people set off on a quest to the Red Rock Mountains, let alone to bring back a dragon.

Suddenly three trumpets sounded and Lord Dashwood appeared on the battlements of the gatehouse. The crowd gathered below him cheered. He put up his hands and made a short speech about the dangers ahead. When he had finished, the crowd cheered again.

The portcullis was raised and the drawbridge was lowered across the moat. Robyn-in-the-Hat led the way on her fine black horse. Soon all that could be heard was the clatter of hooves on the wooden bridge.

But Stubborn the mule refused to move. Everyone stopped.

They tried pushing.

They tried pulling.

They even tried carrots.

In the end, Stubborn the mule did follow the others, but only if Friendly walked alongside her, whispering kind words into her ear.

With the Green Men gone, Lord Dashwood
strode down the spiral stone stairway of the
gatehouse. Able Morris was close behind.

"Now they're out of the way, we can get
down to the really important matters!" he said.

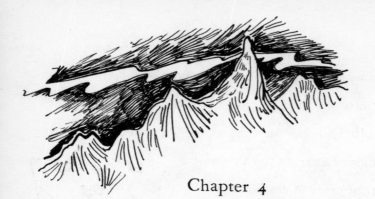

Chapter 4

OFF THE BEATEN TRACK

The first week of the dragon quest was a bit of a let-down. Tom and the others were keen to get to the mountains but that was a matter of putting one foot – or hoof – in front of the other, hour after hour, day after day. They passed through farms and towns and villages

and were made welcome wherever they went. Because they were going about the countryside on official business, they were carrying a standard bearing the Dashwood coat of arms. A standard is a kind of flag. The Dashwood coat of arms was a special design unique to the Dashwood family, and included a pure white unicorn. Lord Dashwood's

knights had it painted on their shields and wore it over their breastplates or chainmail. That way, everyone knew that they were loyal to Lord Dashwood. Carrying his standard meant that the Green Men went under his protection.

Not that the Green Men needed protection at the worst of times and these were the best.

All of the lords were on friendly terms with each other. There was peace in the land at the time of the dragon quest. There were no divided loyalties or sneaky goings-on.

When the Green Men passed one village, a group of children threw cabbages and parsnips at them. Physic was delighted. He jumped down off his horse and gathered them up in his arms.

"These will make a hearty and nourishing soup!" he declared.

At that moment a farmer appeared and grabbed one of the children, hauling him away by the ear. The others ran off, laughing, as fast as their legs could carry them.

Apart from that, the only other piece of real excitement was on the fourth day. That was when some ruffians were foolish enough to try to rob them. But before the fools knew what was happening, Big Jim had knocked two of them over with his staff. Physic was sitting on a third, Squat was biting the knee of a fourth, and three others were being tied up by the other Green Men. All of them were left in a pile on the roadside – wishing that they had chosen any career other than robbery.

It was when the week was over that things got interesting. It was time to use the maps and get off the beaten track. (A beaten track is a track where all the grass gets beaten flat and the ground gets beaten hard through regular use. The less used a track, the less beaten it is. So now you know!) But now the Green Men wouldn't be following paths at all.

The mountains had been visible in the distance for much of their journey. They were still far off, but were beginning to look that much closer. Now Tom believed that they really were getting nearer. He could see the redness of the rocks that gave the mountains their name.

That night they all made camp in what the map referred to as "Ye Wild Woods", but which was little more than a big clump of trees. (Tom could read quite a few words and write his own name, which few people could back then.)

Physic prepared a meal over the campfire and the others stared into the flames. As usual, the talk turned to dragons. Would they find one? How big might it be? How would they capture it? How would the get it back to the castle?

"Grubs up!" said Physic, leaning over the flames to give the big, blackened cooking pot a final stir.

"Excellent," said Big Jim. "What is it? I'm starving!"

"I just told you," said Physic. "It's grubs. Grub stew!"

Suddenly, Tom didn't feel so hungry.

Grubs was another word for creepy-crawlies. He decided he would rather go to bed hungry.

*

The next day the Green Men reached the foothills of the mountains. There was much excitement and cheering and Physic handed everyone an extra bun to celebrate. He had made them a while back, so they were quite stale. Very stale. In fact, they were almost as hard as some of the small red rocks scattered about them.

"I nearly broke a tooth!" Big Jim complained. He threw his bun at Physic. Luckily it missed him. It could have done the ex-outlaw some serious damage.

"They're not that bad," said Friendly, kindly. The truth be told, he couldn't get his teeth into his bun either.

"Forget the buns!" shouted Squat. "What's that?" He pointed half way up the mountain.

Tom tried to figure out exactly where the smallest of the Green Men was pointing. He couldn't see anything at first. Just plenty of boulders and a few trees. Then he saw it: a puff of smoke.

"There must be someone up there ahead of us," said Tom.

"Or some*thing*," groaned Fidget, fidgeting uncomfortably. "That could be dragon smoke."

Big Jim called over Dredwich.

"Could that be dragon's breath?" Big Jim

asked, pointing at the smoke.

"It could be," said the so-called dragon expert. At first, he sounded doubtful. Then he sounded more enthusiastic. "I mean, most probably. In truth, most definitely. Indeed! A very fine example. Typical, in fact."

"So we can take that as a yes?" said Tom.

"Yes," said Dredwich from inside the hood of his cloak. "We're definitely on the right track."

"Come on, then," said Big Jim, gathering up his belongings. "Let's catch ourselves a dragon!"

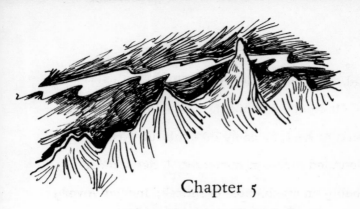

Chapter 5

WHERE BE DRAGONS?

Now, you know that there are dragons in this story and I know that there are dragons in this story because there's the word "dragons" in the title. But the Green Men of Gressingham couldn't find any. They searched for days. And nights. They climbed high into the mountains and deep into the valleys. They searched caves and looked behind big boulders. Dredwich kept on finding "clues" that none of the others could see or understand. He led them here, there and everywhere for days on end.

And what did they find? Nothing. Not a sausage. (And Physic would have been pleased with a sausage or two. They were running out of supplies.)

In the end, Robyn-in-the-Hat called them all together. "We have done our best," she said. "No one can do more. It is time to return to Lord Dashwood empty handed."

Tom was feeling down-hearted. He had failed his first quest.

"Not to worry," said Dredwich, who still seemed quite cheerful. "If there were any dragons here we would have found them. I am sure Lord Dashwood will understand that. It will be good to get back to Dashwood Castle."

"I can't say that I mind not having come face to face with a fire-breathing man-eating monster," Squat confessed.

"Call yourself an outlaw?" Big Jim boomed.

"An in-law," Lanky reminded him. "We act within the law now."

Everyone put a brave face on it, but the Green Men began their long trek home with heavy hearts.

Physic and Friendly collected a few of the strange small round boulders  which littered the mountainside. Each was about the size and shape of a football (when someone finally got around to inventing the game hundreds of years later).

"What do you want those for?" asked Tom.

'They'll make good souvenirs,' said Friendly.

"And they are proof that we actually went to the Red Rock Mountains," Squat added. The rocks were certainly a very strange red colour.

"And few people can claim to have been to these mountains and come back safely," agreed Big Jim. The thought seemed to cheer him up a little.

"And I've made a map of everywhere we went," said Tom. "That's never been done before either."

"So, we've much to be proud of, even though we're not returning with an actual dragon," said Robyn, trying to sound as positive as possible.

Their journey back to

Dashwood Castle was even more uneventful than their journey to the Red Rock Mountains. Most of the villages they passed were strangely empty. When, days later, Dashwood Castle came into view, there was no welcoming committee to greet them.

"I'm glad about that," said Fidget, fidgeting in his saddle. "The fewer people who see us come back without a dragon, the better."

"I shall ride ahead and tell Lord Dashwood of your failure," said Dredwich.

"Our failure?" said Big Jim. "You failed too, Dredwich."

"And you're the expert," muttered Physic.

"Er, yes. Quite," said Dredwich. He dug his heels into the flanks of his horse and galloped off to the castle.

When the rest of the party arrived back at the castle, they were in for a surprise. As they went through the gatehouse into the castle courtyard they couldn't believe their eyes. There were flags and banners and pennants everywhere. Dashwood Castle had been dressed in its greatest finery. The hooves of their horses were silenced by a thick sort of carpet, laid over

the cobblestones. Lord Dashwood himself was hurrying down the outer steps from his private apartments.

"Welcome! Welcome!" He beamed. He stretched his arms open wide.

Robyn-in-the-Hat jumped off her fine black horse and bowed. "Dredwich has told you that we failed, my lord?" she asked.

Lord Dashwood smiled. "You did not fail me," he said. "It is more that Dredwich succeeded."

"I don't understand, Uncle Alf," said Tom.

"The quest for a dragon was a wild goose chase ... Nothing more than a trick to get you away from the castle."

"Wild geese?" said Tom. "You mean you didn't really want a dragon?"

"I would love a dragon, but I'm not even sure that they exist," said his uncle.

"But what about your dragon expert, sire?" asked Robyn.

"Dredwich? He is no dragon expert. He is my friend Lord Hankey's gardener! I had him play the part."

Gardener, thought Tom. That explained the smell of mushrooms and the trail of soil. "But why did you want us out of the way, Uncle?" he asked.

"So that we could make preparations."

"Preparations? Preparations for what, my lord?" asked Big Jim.

"For your reward for saving me from the clutches of the evil Marshal Guppy," said Lord Dashwood.

"Are you going to throw another banquet, sire?" asked Physic. He had fond memories of the last one.

"There will be much feasting, Physic. You can be sure of that. But I want to reward you all in a more lasting way, now that I am fully well again."

"How, Uncle?" asked Tom.

"You, my dear nephew, are to be made a squire. You will no longer be a humble page boy. You have worked hard and earned the title."

Tom glowed with pride.

"The rest of you –" Lord Dashwood paused and looked at Big Jim, Physic, Fidget, Squat, Lanky and the others. "You are to become my knights."

The Green Men all gasped as one.

"Lords, ladies, townsfolk and villagers have been travelling far and wide to be here for the ceremony, which will take place tomorrow. I –"

He was interrupted by a cry from Friendly as he ran into the courtyard. He had been walking alongside Stubborn the mule, who had been weighed down by the round red rocks they had taken as souvenirs from the mountains. They had only just entered the castle, a long way behind the others.

"One's hatching!" Friendly cried.

"Hatching?" asked Tom.

"Hatching!" cried Friendly. He was holding up one of the football-shaped red rocks. It did, indeed, appear to be hatching.

A moment later, the top of the rock broke

off and out poked the head of a tiny dragon.

Yes.

Out poked the head of a tiny dragon.

Now it was everyone's turn to gasp.

The little dragon flapped its stubby wings

and flew up into the air. It made a sneezing

sound and flames shot out of its nostrils.

A guard ran through a stone archway.

"They are ALL hatching, your lordship!" he shouted while trying to swat away a number of bat-sized baby dragons.

The baby dragons swooped and looped the loop. They dive-bombed the people in the courtyard below. They sneezed and breathed out fire.

"Aaaah," said Physic. "Aren't they sweet?"

"Aargh!" yelped Tom as one of them burned his bottom with its fiery breath.

Big Jim had tiny dragons flying round his head like a swarm of bees. "We did it, Robyn," he said with a hearty laugh. "We brought back dragons!"

Just then, one of the newly hatched baby red dragons landed on Tom's shoulder and began nibbling his ear.

Lord Dashwood roared with laughter too.

"Only the Green Men of Gressingham could succeed in catching the wild goose on a wild goose chase!" he declared.

*

And so it was that Tom Dashwood became Squire Dashwood and each of the Green Men became a knight: Sir Jim, Sir Physic, Sir Friendly, Sir Squat, Sir Lanky and so on. Lord Dashwood also awarded the men some land to go with their titles. He gave them Gressingham Forest.

Robyn-in-the-Hat did not accept any title or reward. How could she, without revealing her true identity? She already had a title of her own, for all they knew.

The Green Men were sent on many quests

in their new role as knights, but Sir Fidget and Sir Friendly usually stayed behind. They had important duties of their own, along with Stubborn. The two knights and the mule were nursemaids to a clutch of growing youngsters: the famous Red Dragons of Gressingham.

Dear Mrs Hendrix

It's me. Adrian. I'm well again. The whole garden hose accident and tripping over that nurse is nothing but a dim, distant memory. I walk with a slight limp and am afraid to water the plants, but otherwise I'm fine.

I'm having to use my brother Dave's headed letter paper because I don't know what he did with mine.

I'm so pleased that he managed to convince Sir Philip to write the second Gressingham adventure. Now I'm hoping he will write one last adventure for us so that we can print a big book of three.

Would you please ask him? Do tell him that I would be VERY happy to discuss it over a very large lunch.

Thank you. Fingers crossed once again.

Very best wishes

Adrian Don

Adrian Dongle
Publisher

Sir Philip,

Adrian is back. Are you ready for another FREE LUNCH and GRESSINGHAM ADVENTURE?

Dotty

D

I have been thinking about Gressingham and about how fun it would be to have a story set BEFORE Tom Dashwood met Robyn-in-the-Hat and the Green Men. It could be about them getting together to fight Marshal Guppy at the very beginning.

I have also been thinking about what fun it would be to have a tour around a doughnut factory. Do you think Adrian might arrange that instead of lunch?

P.A.

Sir Philip,

The idea of setting a story before the first two sounds great! And well done for remembering Adrian's name. But even I can't see a way of coming up with a good reason for him to take you on a tour of a doughnut factory!!!

Dotty

All right, D.
   Keep your hair on!
                    P.A.

D

I have been thinking about Gressingham and about how fun it would be to have a story set BEFORE Tom Dashwood met H

All right, D.

Keep your hai

ARDAGH HOUSE

Dear Adrian,

Rather than meeting over lunch and discussing ideas for a new book, I have gone ahead and written it.

Here it is. It's called THE BLACK KNIGHT OF GRESSINGHAM, set back in the days when the evil Marshal Guppy first tricks Lord Dashwood into letting him rule in his name.

I hope you enjoy reading it as much as I enjoyed writing it.

All the best,

Philip

P.S. Because we didn't have lunch, could you send me a hamper instead?

The Black Knight of
GRESSINGHAM

There are many tales told of the Green Men of Gressingham, the famous outlaws of Gressingham Forest. About their fight for justice and their brave deeds. About their clever tricks and their brown clothes. You may well know how they finally defeated the evil Marshal Guppy and how they went in search of dragons. But few will have heard the tale of the Black Knight which happened long before these two adventures, back in the early days of the Green Men's fight for what was right.

Chapter 1

THE ONLY MAN FOR THE JOB

The banging on the cottage door was getting louder and louder. But it wasn't really a cottage. It was more of a hovel. And it wasn't really a door. It was more of a number of odd-shaped planks that had been very badly nailed together by someone who wasn't very good at nailing things.

The person who wasn't very good at nailing things was a very small man named Squat. He was in bed and doing his very best to ignore the banging. Poor people didn't have proper beds in those days, especially poor people living in hovels. Squat was lying on a pile of straw, using an old flour sack as a blanket. The sack covered most of him because he was so small.

Squat pulled the sack over his head as the banging got louder. When the banging got even louder, he tried sticking some of the straw from his bed in his ears. It prickled. Squat gave up and decided to open the door. There was no need.

With one last, loud BANG the door finally gave way and fell flat on the hard mud floor of Squat's hovel. It narrowly missed Squat, who jumped to one side.

"Sorry!" boomed a loud voice and in came a

man so tall that he seemed to take up the whole hovel.

"Big Jim!" gasped Squat. He looked at his old friend, who was dressed in the brown clothes of an outlaw. "What are you doing here?"

Big Jim was busy lifting up the door and trying to fix it back in place.

"I'm here because we need your help," said Big Jim.

Big Jim needed his help? How on earth could he help Jim?

"Pull up a stool and sit down," Squat said. (There was only one stool.) He hoped that Big Jim would take up less room sitting down.

So Big Jim sat on the stool. His knees almost came up to his nose. He reminded Squat of the frog in the pond behind his home.

"We need you!" said Big Jim. "We want you to join."

"Join what?" asked Squat. He half-hoped Big Jim would ask him to join two planks of wood together or two pieces of string.

"Join the Green Men of Gressingham!" said Big Jim. "Join us and become an outlaw!"

Squat had feared Jim was going to say that. He was not sure that he was brave enough to be an outlaw.

"Why?" he asked with a gulp. "I can't fire a bow and arrow and I don't know how to fight with a sword or with my fists." Squat knew that the outlaws loved a good fight.

Big Jim looked at his friend.

He made most people look small, but Squat really was tiny. Big Jim towered over Squat even though he was sitting down and Squat was standing.

"We have a special mission and we all agreed that you are the only man for the job," said Big Jim.

"Really?" said Squat. His face went red. This was because he was glowing with pride. Squat didn't often glow with pride. In fact, he had never glowed with pride before. It felt good.

"All of you agreed?" asked Squat (because he wanted to hear Big Jim say it again).

"Yes," said Big Jim. "Even Robyn-in-the-Hat agreed."

Squat found himself glowing with even more pride. Robyn-in-the-Hat was the most famous person for miles around. (And very few people travelled further than miles around in those days.) There were songs sung about her around fires on dark nights. There were tales told and rumours whispered.

Robyn-in-the-Hat was the leader of the Green Men of Gressingham but, unlike the men, she wasn't a poor peasant or a monk. She was a rich lady with sparkling blue eyes. But much of her face was hidden by a strange mask fixed to her hat. She was a living, breathing MYSTERY. (There. I wrote the word in capital letters to show just what a big mystery she was.)

"And what is this special mission you need me for?" asked Squat. He was very excited now.

"I can't tell you," said Big Jim. "I can't tell you unless you agree to become one of us outlaws first!"

"Can I have time to think?" asked Squat, because becoming a Green Man would mean leaving his old life behind. If he were an outlaw then he would even have to leave this hovel that he called home – and the friendly frog at the back.

But time was one thing Squat did not have.

*

Big Jim was about to say something when he was interrupted by a noise. It came from outside.

There was the sound of horses' hooves on hard earth and the chinking of soldiers' chainmail.

These stopped and a voice commanded, "Come out, in the name of Lord Dashwood, peasant!"

Squat was the first to admit that he was a peasant. He was born a peasant and thought that he would die one. But he didn't like the way the voice had said the word "peasant". Whoever was outside his hovel had said "peasant" as if he were a worthless piece of nothing.

But Squat wasn't a worthless piece of nothing. He was a human being with feelings. And, just because he was very small, it did not mean his feelings weren't just as big as everyone else's.

He opened his sort-of-fixed sort-of door and blinked in the morning light. He found himself facing none other than Marshal Guppy. Yes, it

was the evil Marshal
Guppy, the man who
ruled the local lands
in the name of Lord
Dashwood of Dashwood
Castle.

The Marshal was on horseback with two
foot soldiers standing on either side of him. All
four of them looked a little red in the face from
running to keep up with him. And they also
looked a little cross. It wasn't fair. They were
the ones in heavy chainmail and carrying heavy
swords, but he was the one on the horse!

Marshal Guppy raised an eyebrow. "Aha!"
he said. "I was wrong. Not one peasant but two.
And in such a tiny ..." He stared at Squat's hovel
as if he were trying to come up with a word to

describe it. "... space," he said at last. "Come on out, Big Jim. I know you are in there!"

Big Jim didn't need asking twice. He ducked through the small doorway to face his enemy.

"What have we here, little man?" said Guppy to Squat. "You dare to hide an outlaw in your home?"

Before Big Jim or Squat had a chance to say anything, the Marshal nodded at the four soldiers who drew their big, flat swords from their scabbards. (A scabbard is a leather sheath for keeping a sword in.)

"ARREST THEM!" Marshal Guppy commanded.

Two of the soldiers strode towards Big Jim.

The other two strode towards Squat.

This was a big mistake.

All four of them should have gone for
Big Jim.

Big Jim picked up the two soldiers nearest
to him. One in each hand. And he banged their
heads together. There was a loud CLANG and
their helmets fell to the ground and rolled

around on the grass. Then their swords fell from their hands and they toppled forward, groaning.

If this story were a cartoon, the soldiers would have gone cross-eyed, stuck out their tongues, and little tweeting birds would have fluttered around their heads in circles.

Squat snatched one of the swords from the ground. It was very heavy and almost as tall as he was, so he had to hold it in both hands. He waved it around dangerously in front of him. The remaining two soldiers looked nervous.

Meanwhile, Big Jim picked up the other sword, spun it over his head and let it fly. He wasn't aiming at the soldiers but at Marshal Guppy on his horse. The Marshal's eyes widened in horror and surprise. He pulled on his horse's reins, jabbed its flanks with his spurs and galloped off to safety. The sword only just missed him.

The two soldiers who were still standing simply turned and ran.

"Nice work, Squat," said Big Jim, slapping the smaller man on the back as they watched them go.

The slap made Squat drop his sword but he managed not to fall flat on his face. A slap on the back from Big Jim was a bit like being kicked by Nancy, Max the Miller's donkey.

Squat grinned. It wasn't every day that someone gave Marshal Guppy a taste of his own medicine. But he wasn't grinning for long.

"What do we do now?" he asked.

"We tie up these two," said Big Jim. He

dragged the two soldiers to a tree. "Give me a helping hand, will you?"

They sat one soldier up against one side of the tree trunk and the other soldier against the other. Squat fetched a rope and they wrapped it around the men, tying them firmly in place.

"Now you can't stay here even if you wanted to," Big Jim told Squat. "You've stood your ground against Marshal Guppy. You are a wanted man!"

"So now I'm an outlaw if I like it or not!" said Squat.

"Yes," said Big Jim. He bent down and shook Squat's hand. "Welcome to the Green Men of Gressingham."

Chapter 2

BUSINESS TO DISCUSS

It took a while for Squat and Big Jim to reach the Green Men's secret camp. It was hidden deep in Gressingham Forest

Nowadays, there are three main uses for forests:

1. To grow trees for timber and paper.

2. As places where you can have nice country walks and point at things and say, "Ooo! Look at that bird!" or "That's a pretty leaf!"

3. As a place to get exercise by running, cycling or zipping between trees on pulleys and wire walkways.

Back in the days of the Green Men, important families lived in castles and ruled their lands the way the kings ruled their countries. And much of those lands were covered by forests. Those forests were very busy places, much busier than nowadays. People went foraging for food for themselves and for their animals. Men, women and children gathered mushrooms and berries and sweet chestnuts.

Pigs snuffled about for tasty acorns. Folk collected fire wood. They burned charcoal. They cut twigs from willow trees to weave baskets and make furniture. And the rich hunted stags and wild boar.

So the Green Men's secret camp needed to be somewhere off the beaten track. It was near enough to a stream, but not too close to be soggy. And it had an excellent look out tree.

As Big Jim and Squat arrived, two Green Men slid out of the tree and landed in front of them. They were called Fidget and Friendly and they hit the ground at the same time with a single THUMP!

"You came!" said Fidget.

"I didn't have much choice!" said Squat with a grin almost as big as his face. He'd been friends with Fidget before Fidget had joined the outlaws. They used to work together in Lord Dashwood's fields.

"Did you have to twist his arm?" Friendly asked Big Jim.

"Marshal Guppy helped you make up your mind, didn't he, Squat?" said Big Jim with a smile.

Friendly gave a friendly laugh. "That was very nice of him. What happened?"

Big Jim and Squat told them as they walked into the camp. In the middle of the camp was a bubbling cauldron of soup cooking over an open fire. It was being lovingly stirred by the plump monk called Physic.

Physic had the strange haircut of a monk and was not dressed quite like the others. He wore monk's clothes, which are called a habit.

His habit was made from the same brown material as all the other Green Men's outfits.

Next to the monk stood none other than Robyn-in-the-Hat herself.

Squat suddenly felt all nervous and shy. He was not only in front of a Gressingham legend but also a real lady.

He didn't stay nervous for long. Robyn threw her arms around Squat and lifted him off his feet. His legs kicked in the air. "Thank you for

joining us, brave Squat!" she said. She kissed him on the top of his head before putting him back down again. "Now, we have business to discuss."

Squat could not believe how quickly his life had changed. He had gone to bed a peasant ready to work on Lord Dashwood's land the next morning. But when the next morning came, he'd turned into an outlaw!

"Gather the men, Jim," said Robyn-in-the-Hat. Soon everyone but two lookouts was sitting in the clearing in the middle of the outlaws' camp.

"As most of you know," said Robyn, "Marshal Guppy has a new weapon in his fight against good. This weapon is a man. He is a knight. He is a Frenchman. He is Sir Jacques de Zack. He will fight for any man and for any

thing in return for gold. And Marshal
Guppy is paying him very well
indeed."

"I saw Sir Jacques at a
jousting match last month," said Big
Jim. "He knocked his opponent off his
horse with the first charge of his lance.
Then he hacked him with his sword
and beat him with his mace and
morning star in hand-to-hand combat on foot. He
showed no mercy. He was a terrifying fighting
machine!"

"I remember the time that Sam the
Shepherd was sending his flock across the wooden
bridge at Washford," Friendly said. "Sir Jacques
wanted to ride across the bridge the other way.
The evil knight galloped through the sheep,

hacking at the frightened animals as he went."

There were boos and hisses from the Green Men. They did not like to hear about animals being treated badly. Friendly patted Martha the pig. (She had smelled the soup and had come to investigate.)

"The people of Gressingham are frightened enough with all these new laws, taxes and rules coming from Dashwood Castle," said Robyn. "Now things are even worse with Marshal Guppy having this terrifying law-enforcer as his right-hand man. We must make sure that Sir Jacques de Zack goes back to France and stays there. And this is where you come in, Squat."

"Me?" said Squat, who was sitting cross-legged at her feet. He was not quite sure he'd heard her right. "But how?"

"There are not many ways to stop a man like Sir Jacques," said Robyn. "We could kill him –"

"But we do not believe in killing," Big Jim explained.

"We could try defeating him so soundly that he is too ashamed to show his face around here again –" said Robyn.

"But who can defeat such a powerful knight as him?" said Big Jim.

"Or we could scare him away," said Robyn.

"And scaring him away is where you get to play your part, Squat," said Big Jim with a big grin.

Squat gasped. "Me scare away the best and meanest knight in the land? But how?"

Chapter 3

A CHANGE OF PLAN

Marshal Guppy was in a bad mood. He was in more than a bad mood. He was furious. He rode up to the edge of the dark green moat surrounding Dashwood Castle. He couldn't get across because the drawbridge was up.

"Let me enter!" he shouted.

"Who goes there?" a guard called down from the battlements of the gatehouse tower.

"Me!" screamed Guppy. "Now let me in!"

"Who's me –?" began the guard, peering over the battlement.

"IT'S MARSHAL GUPPY AND IF YOU DON'T LOWER THE DRAWBRIDGE THIS INSTANT, I AM GOING TO HAVE YOU THROWN INTO THE MOAT. THEN, IF YOU DON'T DROWN, I WILL HAVE YOU THROWN INTO THE DEEPEST DUNGEON WHERE YOU WILL BE HUNG UPSIDE-DOWN BY YOUR ANKLES FOR A YEAR AND A DAY … DO I MAKE MYSELF CLEAR?"

"Yes, sire!" said the guard. Although he was used to the Marshal's rages, he had never seen Guppy quite so red in the face before. The drawbridge lowered.

The front of the drawbridge barely had time to touch the ground before Marshal Guppy was galloping his horse across it, through the main gate and into the courtyard. The horse's hooves made a loud clattering noise on the cobbles.

"RAMBLE?" shouted Guppy, as he swung down to the ground.

"Yes, sire?" said a tall, thin man stepping out of the shadows.

Guppy looked calmer when he saw him. You might even say he looked happier. "Have Sir Jacques de Zack meet me in my private chamber," he ordered.

"Right away, sire," said Ramble, the Commander of the Guards, with a nod.

Guppy strode across the courtyard, then ducked through a doorway and up the spiral stone staircase that led to his own private chambers. He threw open the door, marched across the wooden floor and flung himself on his bed.

He couldn't stop thinking about Big Jim throwing that sword at him and making him turn and flee. "NO ONE MAKES A FOOL OUT OF GUPPY!" he shouted to himself.

A startled dove that had been sleeping on the window ledge flew high up into the sky. The flap of its wings made Guppy jump and feel rather foolish.

There was a knock at the door and in strode the fine figure of Sir Jacques de Zack. He was clanking as he walked because he was fully dressed in his gleaming silver armour, apart from his helmet.

"Do you even sleep in your armour?" Guppy

laughed.

"I will if you pay me to," said Sir Jacques

with his French accent. "A good knight must

always be prepared and ready for battle!"

"But you are a bad knight," said Marshal Guppy with an evil sneer.

"I think you mean a bad man, Marshal," said Sir Jacques. "I am bad because I do not fight for what is right but for who pays the most ... but I fight well. Perhaps that makes me a good bad knight!"

Now both men laughed in a rather nasty way.

"I saw Big Jim on the outskirts of the village today. The outlaw," Guppy told Sir Jacques. "Those Green Men are getting bolder and cause me more trouble every day. I want you to take as many men as you need to flush them out and finish them off once and for all."

"When you say 'finish them off', Marshal, what exactly do you mean?" asked the

Frenchman. "I do not want there to be any misunderstanding."

"Of course not, Sir Jacques. What I mean is that I want you to crush them. To stamp on them. TO SNUFF THEM OUT LIKE A CANDLE."

"That would be my pleasure, Marshal," said Sir Jacques de Zack with a bow.

"All except their leader Robyn-in-the-Hat," the marshal added. "I want her brought back here as my prisoner. Then I can unmask her and reveal her true identity."

"Very good, Marshal," said Sir Jacques. "Or do I mean very bad? I must go and make plans at once." He turned and clanked back towards the door. "When shall I pay my unannounced visit to the Green Men of Gressingham?"

"Tomorrow," said Guppy.

"Tomorrow?" said Sir Jacques. He stopped in his tracks. The smile fell from his face. "*Non, non, non.* Tomorrow is not possible."

"You need more time?" demanded Marshal Guppy. His anger was rising again.

"It is not that," said Sir Jacques. "I have studied the phases of the Moon. To attack tomorrow would be a very bad omen. I will not do it."

Marshal Guppy sighed. He knew that there was no point in arguing with the Frenchman when it came to superstitions. Sir Jacques was famous for being superstitious. His chamber was full of Moon charts, star charts and good luck charms. This was a small price for Marshal Guppy to pay for having such a demon fighter on his side.

"Very well," he said. "You will hunt down the outlaws on Saturday ... unless you object to fighting at the weekend?"

"Non, non, non. The weekend is not a problem. It will be my pleasure," said the Frenchman. "Soon the Green Men will be no more."

Chapter 4

A BRAVE HEART

The newest and smallest member of the
Green Men of Gressingham was made
welcome by the others. It helped that Squat
did not say "No!" or run and hide when Robyn
explained the basics of the plan to defeat Sir
Jacques and the part he would have to play. It
was not a plan without its dangers.

"Will you do it?" she asked.

"Of course!" said Squat. He did not feel as

brave as he may have sounded. The other Green Men cheered.

"Would now be a good time for soup?" asked Physic (who thought that any time was a good time for eating). The soup contained the finest roots from the forest floor.

"An excellent time for soup!" said Robyn-in-the-Hat.

There was another loud cheer and a clatter of wooden soup bowls and spoons as the men lined up to be fed.

Robyn-in-the-Hat stepped forward. She put her hand on Squat's shoulder. "I must leave now and get back to my other duties in my other life, but I will return at sundown." She looked at him with her sparkling blue eyes through the mask. "You are a small man with a brave heart and a big part in our plan," she said. "Thank you for joining our number, Squat. We must find you an outlaw's uniform as soon as we can."

One of the outlaws led over Robyn's horse. She jumped into the saddle and galloped off between the trees with a wave.

Physic thrust a bowl of soup into Squat's hands. Squat sat on a fallen log to eat it with Big Jim on one side of him and Friendly on the other.

"I must measure you up for a fitting," said Friendly. "And not just for your brown clothes."

When the soup was eaten, Big Jim led Squat over to the western edge of the outlaws' camp. Here there was a rocky hillside, dotted with scrubby plants and bushes.

"Up here!" said Big Jim, leaping up the hillside and waiting by a large, thorny bush with sharp, pointy leaves.

Squat scrambled up after him. Big Jim pulled aside the bush to reveal the opening to a cave. He ducked inside and Squat followed. Daylight from a hole high up in the rocky roof lit parts of the cave, but much of it was still in shadow.

"What an amazing place!" said Squat in wonder.

"Yes," said Big Jim. "Even if our enemies were to discover our camp, this cave would remain an excellent hiding place."

Suddenly the hairs on the back of Squat's neck began to prickle. He got the strange feeling that they were not alone. He spun around and looked into the shadows.

He caught the glint of something metal.

He peered deeper into the murky corners and gasped.

Squat could make out the figure of a huge knight in jet-black armour gripping an enormous sword.

The following morning was as sunny as the last. The birds were singing. The castle servants had been up for hours. It was Friday and Sir Jacques de Zack did not want to leave anything to chance. His charts had made it very clear that today would not be a good day.

"Should I stay indoors or go outside?" he asked his squire (whose job it was to look after him).

"It might be safer to stay indoors, sire," said the squire, who was used to his master's superstitious ways.

"But the roof may fall in and crush me or I may fall down the stairs and break my neck!" said Sir Jacques.

"Then you might be safer outdoors," said the squire.

"But I may have a bad fall from my horse or be trampled by cows."

"Then indoors would be better," said the squire.

"But a knocked-over candle may set fire to a wall-hanging and trap me in a sheet of flame!"

"Then outdoors?"

"Where a flash flood may sweep me away into a swollen river and wash me out to sea."

And so the conversation went, backwards and forwards, backwards and forwards for a good ten minutes.

You may have noticed that not one of Sir Jacques de Zack's fears involved other people. One thing the Frenchman was never afraid of *was* people. He had no reason to be. He would fight anyone. And he never lost a fight.

Sir Jacques decided his best bet was to stay indoors and make plans for the next day's sport: the hunt for the Green Men of Gressingham.

And the next day came soon enough, as next days do.

Sir Jacques clattered across the cobbled courtyard on his fine horse. The drawbridge was lowered and he cantered out of Dashwood Castle. There, waiting for him, were a dozen other knights on horseback and a small army of foot soldiers.

"Today we have just one aim," Sir Jacques de Zack announced. "We are going to rid Gressingham of those thieves and murderers who call themselves outlaws. None but their leader

Robyn-in-the-Hat must remain alive. They have been a thorn in Lord Dashwood's side for too long."

"But what of a trial, Sir Jacques?" said one of the knights. "Surely we should capture them and –?"

"Then hang them?" Sir Jacques interrupted. "Why waste time? The sentence will be death anyway. Let us be judge and executioner! Come!"

Chapter 5

OFF HIS HEAD

The quickest way for Sir Jacques de Zack and his men to reach Gressingham Forest was to cross a stone bridge at a place called Stonebridge Crossing. (You can probably guess how it got its name.)

When they reached it, they found the way blocked. A man was sitting on his horse in the very middle of the bridge. The horse was huge. It was the size of a carthorse used for pulling heavy wagons. And the man? He looked huge too. It was impossible to see his face. He was covered from head to toe in black armour. He clutched a sword in his right gauntlet. Its blade was not silver, but was also as black as night.

"Let me pass, Black Knight, in the name of Lord Dashwood!" shouted Sir Jacques de Zack. He was lying, of course. Poor Lord Dashwood knew nothing of what he and Marshal Guppy were doing.

The Black Knight said nothing.

"I said, let me past!" the Frenchman repeated. "We have rats to catch!"

"You shall not pass," boomed the Black Knight in reply.

"Is that a threat?" said Sir Jacques, his mouth curling into a sneer.

"It is a promise," said the Black Knight.

Sir Jacques de Zack was a happy man. He had been challenged to fight by a fellow knight. This man in black looked to be a worthy opponent. He would enjoy defeating him.

"You think you can stop me and my men from crossing that bridge?" shouted the Frenchman. "We could hack you down with our swords in an instant."

"You could, sir," said the Black Knight, his voice booming. "But my challenge is that the fight is one to one, man to man."

"Just you and I?" said Sir Jacques.

"Just you and I," said the Black Knight, his helmet nodding. "And, if I win, your men will turn back and return to Dashwood Castle."

"Very well," said Sir Jacques. "But you will not win." He turned to face his men. "You heard the challenge," he said. "I fight this black knight and if he wins –" The Frenchman laughed. "– then you all return to the castle."

Before the final words had left his mouth, Sir Jacques was galloping his horse towards the bridge. He had his sword outstretched in front of him.

Apart from slowly raising his own sword, the Black Knight did not move. He sat in his saddle as if he didn't have a care in the world.

Sir Jacques charged his horse up the arch of the bridge, right into the middle so that he was in front of the Black Knight. With a roar like a wild animal, he brought his sword crashing down on his enemy.

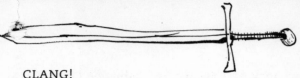

CLANG!

The other knights watched in a mixture of horror and amazement as the Black Knight's head seemed to separate from his body with a single slash of Sir Jacques' huge broadsword. It went spinning through the air in its helmet and splashed into the river below.

The headless body stayed sitting on the horse, still gripping the huge black sword.

After a moment of stunned silence, Sir Jacques' men cheered. He pulled off his helmet and began riding back to them. Then he heard the sound of hooves behind him.

Sir Jacques turned to see the headless Black Knight riding towards him. Now the Black Knight's arm was outstretched and his sword was raised.

"Prepare to die!" boomed the Black Knight.

Sir Jacques did not stop to wonder how a headless man could speak.

Or ride a horse.

Or raise a sword.

He did not stop to wonder because he knew that the Black Knight was no ordinary man.

He was a devil. No lucky charm could save him now.

"Retreat! Flee!" wailed the terrified Frenchman, digging his spurs into his horse's flanks and galloping past his men into the distance. Now they too turned and fled.

As soon as the last of Sir Jacques de Zack and his men had disappeared from view, the sound of laughter filled Stonebridge Crossing.

Green Men appeared from their leafy

hiding places, dropping from the trees like ripe and rather brown fruit. Many of them clutched bows and arrows.

Physic the monk was too plump to climb trees and so he had hidden under straw in an old cart with a broken wheel. He sat up, spitting some straw from his mouth.

Big Jim had been hiding in the river under the arch of the bridge. He waded out of the water and helped Physic out of the cart.

Now they all gathered around the headless Black Knight, still on top of his huge horse. Big Jim banged on his tummy. "Are you all right in there, Squat?" he asked.

"I will be if you stop banging!" said Squat. "You're giving me a headache."

His voice still sounded loud and deep as it

boomed inside the armour.

The Green Men roared with laughter.

Meanwhile, Friendly had fished the Black Knight's helmet out of the river. It had a head in it all right. A head of cabbage to make the helmet heavy.

The others helped Squat off the horse and out of the armour that he filled so little of. Perhaps this picture will explain it best.

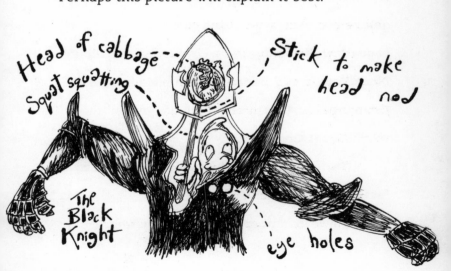

Head of cabbage

Squat squatting

Stick to make head nod

The Black Knight

eye holes

When Squat's feet were firmly back on the ground, Big Jim handed him the Black Knight's sword. Not that there ever really was a Black Knight, of course, just a large suit of armour with a very small man and a cabbage inside.

Squat took the sword and waved it wildly above his head. The Green Men cheered. It was a piece of wood, cut into a sword shape and painted black. There was no way Squat would have been able to lift his heavy armour-covered arm and a heavy metal sword.

"Few, if any, unarmed men have faced Sir Jacques de Zack in combat and lived to tell the tale!" said Friendly.

"Not just lived to tell the tale but to have made him flee, scared for his life!" said Robyn-in-the-Hat. She seemed to have appeared out of nowhere.

That night there was
much singing and drinking and
laughter around the outlaws'
campfire in Gressingham Forest.
The Green Men all raised their
drinking cups to their new
hero, the brave Black Knight
of Gressingham.

And what of the
superstitious Sir Jacques de Zack? He jumped on
a boat straight back France, gave all his gold to
the poor, and tried to be a good man for the rest
of his days.

And what of Marshal Guppy? Well, he was
furious. Which should come as no surprise. (He
did a lot more SHOUTING.)

And what does this tale teach us? That good

triumphs over evil? Not always. But it does show us that some fights are won with brains, even if you have a cabbage for a head.

And so ends the final tale in this book, but the first adventure of the Green Men of Gressingham. Are there other tales to tell of Robyn-in-the Hat and her band of merry outlaws? Of course there are. And of their later quests when they became loyal knights to Tom Dashwood's Uncle Alf? Yup. And what of Tom himself? Did he himself become a knight? Well, that's certainly another story.

The End

conkers